go with me

go with me

CASTLE FREEMAN

DUCKWORTH OVERLOOK

First published in the UK in 2009 by

Duckworth Overlook
30 Calvin Street, London, E1 6NW
Tel: 020 7490 7300
info@duckworth-publishers.co.uk
www.ducknet.co.uk

For bulk and special sales
please contact sales@duckworth-publishers.co.uk

This edition first published in 2016

A catalogue record for this book is available
from the British Library

Interior design by Megan Jones Design

9780715650455

for
CHRISTINA WARD

CONTENTS

"Marvel have I," said the damsel, "what manner of man ye be, for it may never be other but that ye be come of gentle blood, for so foully and shamefully did never woman revile a knight as I have done you, and ever courteously ye have suffered me, and that comes never but of gentle blood."

— SIR THOMAS MALORY,
Le Morte d'Arthur,
"The Tale of Sir Gareth of Orkney"

1

EARLY RISERS

Midsummer: The long days begin in bright, rising mist and never end. Their hours stretch, they stretch. They stretch to hold everything you can shove into them; they'll take whatever you've got. Action, no action, good ideas, bad ideas, talk, love, trouble, every kind of lie — they'll hold them all. Work? No. Nobody works any longer. To be sure, they did. The farmers worked. The midsummer days were the best working time of the year for the farmers, but the farmers are gone. They worked, they built, but they're gone. Who's next?

Sheriff Ripley Wingate, an early riser, turned off the road and into the lot behind the courthouse. Not yet seven. The morning fog still hung to the ground, a heavy gray curtain. It shifted, wavered, passed in woolly swags and swirls, parted. Nearly hidden in the mist, in a corner of the lot, another vehicle, a little car, empty.

The sheriff parked his truck in his spot near the court building and walked across the lot to the car, an Escort with its rear window partly broken out and covered with a plastic sheet and tape. He approached the passenger's side and bent to look inside the car. Not empty. A young woman was curled up in the driver's seat, asleep. Her knees were pulled up behind the steering wheel; her head rested against the window. On the passenger's seat beside her was a kitchen knife with a blade maybe four inches long, and in the rear seat a furry bundle the sheriff couldn't quite make out. He tapped lightly on the window.

The sleeping woman opened her eyes. She looked around her, then saw the sheriff at the window. She started. She drew back against her door, watching him. Her right hand went to the little knife on the seat beside her.

"Help you?" Sheriff Wingate asked her.

"I'm waiting for the sheriff," the young woman said.

"What?"

"I'm waiting for the sheriff," the young woman said again, louder, to be heard through the closed windows of the little car.

"I'm the sheriff."

"You are?"

"Why don't you come on inside?" the sheriff said. He nodded toward the courthouse.

The young woman made no move to leave the car, but she leaned across the seat and rolled the passenger's window down a couple of inches.

"You don't have a uniform," she said.

"No," the sheriff said. He straightened and turned to start back to the courthouse.

"How do I know you're the sheriff?"

"I don't know what to tell you," the sheriff said. "You can sit out here long as you want. Maybe another sheriff will come along."

"Wait," said the young woman. She uncurled herself from the seat, opened the door, and stood beside her car. She was tall and wore her brown hair long, very long, in a soft fall that hung down her back past her shoulder blades. The sheriff watched her. She didn't look drunk, she didn't act drunk, she didn't smell drunk. She closed the car door and looked across its roof at him.

"All right," she said.

The sheriff waited for her, letting her go ahead of him.

"You first," said the young woman.

The sheriff shook his head. "I ain't the one with the knife," he said. "You are. You go in front."

"Oh," said the young woman. The kitchen knife lay on the seat of her car. She left it and started toward the courthouse, with the sheriff following her.

In his tiny office in the basement of the courthouse Sheriff Wingate pointed to a chair in front of his desk, and the young woman sat. He let her sit for a minute, let her settle, while he fussed. He started the coffee machine, he tore yesterday's page from his calendar and tossed it into the wastepaper basket. He turned the volume on the radio scanner up, then down. Then he sat behind his desk, facing the young woman.

"What can we do for you?" the sheriff asked her.

"I need help," the young woman said.

"Help with what?"

"He's after me," she said. "A man. He wants to hurt me."

"A man?"

"That's right. He watches me. He follows me. He won't let me alone."

"Blackway," the sheriff said.

"You know about this?"

"I know Blackway," the sheriff said. "Most around here do. Coffee?" He rose and went to the coffee machine.

The young woman shook her head.

The sheriff poured himself a cup of coffee and returned to his chair.

"Blackway's following you?" he asked.

"That's what I said."

"For how long?"

"A week, ten days," the young woman said. "He watches me. Like one time, I was coming out of a lot. He pulled in front of me, cut me off. He just sat there, in that big truck he has. Looking at me. Letting me see him looking at me. Then he went away. He'd done that before. Then he smashed in the window of my car."

"You were there when he did that?" the sheriff asked her. "You saw him?"

"No. It happened at night. I was asleep, the car was parked."

"Anybody else see him, you know about?"

"No."

"So you can't say for sure he did it."

"He did it," the young woman said. "Who else would?"

"Maybe nobody," said the sheriff. "Maybe a lot of people. What else?"

Now the young woman swallowed hard. She looked at the floor, shook her head. She tried to answer, swallowed again.

"Take it easy," said the sheriff.

"Annabelle," the young woman said at last. "He got Annabelle. He came to my place and he got her."

"Annabelle?"

"My cat. He killed her."

The sheriff nodded. "You had her in the backseat," he said.

"Last night," the young woman said. "I found her on my front steps. Her throat was cut. Her head was almost cut off."

"Take it easy," said the sheriff.

The young woman swallowed, looked at the floor. She nodded.

"Have a cup of coffee," the sheriff said.

The young woman nodded again.

The sheriff got up from his chair and went to the coffee machine. He poured out a cup for the young woman.

"Milk and sugar?"

"Sugar."

The sheriff put a spoonful of sugar into her cup and stirred her coffee. He brought the cup to the desk and set it down in front of her. The young woman picked it up and held it in both her hands, as though her hands were cold. Long, slim hands.

The sheriff returned to his chair. He sat.

"So you packed up the cat and came over here in the middle of the night," he said.

"Yes."

"If Blackway showed up, you were going to stick him with your fruit knife."

"It's better than nothing," said the young woman.

"Is it?" the sheriff asked her. "You been waiting out there all night?"

"Yes."

"Why?"

The young woman looked at him.

"Why?" she said. "What do you mean, why? I told you why. I'm scared. I'm being threatened. Stalked. I'm being stalked. You're the law. I need protection. I need you to help me. I need you to do something."

"Do what?"

"What?" the young woman said. "I don't know. Something.

Look, you're the law, not me. And no, I can't prove he killed Annabelle. I didn't see him do it. I know he did it."

"I ain't saying he didn't."

"All right, then," said the young woman. "What can you do?"

"Not much."

"Not much?"

"I could go see him, I guess," the sheriff said. "Blackway. I could have a talk with him, I guess. I don't know if that would make things better, though. Do you? I expect it would make them worse. Knowing Blackway."

"He wants to hurt me," said the young woman. "He's going to hurt me. That's where he's going with this."

Sheriff Wingate looked at her levelly. He nodded.

"I can't arrest him for what he wants to do," he said. "That ain't the way it works. That ain't the law. You know it ain't."

"Don't tell me what I know," said the young woman.

"That ain't the way it works," the sheriff went on, "and that ain't the way you want it to work."

"Don't tell me what I want."

The sheriff didn't reply. He looked across the desk at the young woman. He waited.

"Listen," the young woman said. She set her coffee cup down on the desk. "Didn't you hear me? He killed my cat. My fucking cat. He cut her fucking throat. So don't tell me what I want." She started to leave her chair.

"Sit down," the sheriff said.

The young woman looked at him across the desk. She sat again.

"Why?" she asked. "Why should I sit down? You're telling me you can't do anything. You're telling me I have to wait till he does something, till he gets to me, kills me, before you can do anything."

"You could put it that way, I guess," the sheriff said.

"How would you put it?"

"That way."

"Well, then," said the young woman, and again she half rose from her chair.

"Sit," said the sheriff. "Have you got any people around? Any family?"

"No. Nobody."

"Where are you from?"

"Upstate."

"Go home," said the sheriff.

"No."

"Why not?"

"Look," the young woman said, "I haven't done anything, here. Blackway has. Let Blackway go home."

"Blackway is home," said the sheriff.

They sat in silence for a moment.

"You have friends?" the sheriff asked the young woman. "Anybody? Down here, I mean? You were going with Russell Bay's boy. With Kevin, weren't you?"

"Kevin's gone," said the young woman. "He took off. He ran out. I don't have anybody else. I mean, I don't know anybody else. And if I did, so what? You're telling me nobody can help me, right?"

"I'm telling you the law can't help you," said the sheriff. "That ain't quite the same thing, is it?"

The young woman sat back in her chair. She was listening to him now.

"No," she said. "No, it's not."

"You know the mill?" the sheriff asked her. "Other side of town, big old place right on the road? Used to be the chair shop?"

"The chair company? I've seen the sign."

"You might go there," the sheriff said. "There's usually a few fellows around there. Ask for Whizzer. Do you know him?"

"Whizzer?"

"Ask for Whizzer. Tell him I said you should go there. Tell him about Blackway. Ask him if Scotty's around."

"Scotty?"

"Scotty Cavanaugh," said the sheriff. "He knows Blackway. He and Blackway have had dealings, you could say. Scotty might be able to help you with this thing."

"Help me, how?"

"That would be up to him," the sheriff said. "Wouldn't it?"

"What if he won't?"

"He will if Whizzer asks him to."

"Who's Whizzer?" the young woman asked.

"Oh, Whizzer's kind of like the boss, down there," said Sheriff Wingate. "It's his place. Go see him. See Whizzer."

2

THE DEAD RIVER CHAIR COMPANY

Alonzo Boot, the one they called Whizzer, awoke on the couch. He often spent the night there. No reason to go to bed. He didn't sleep much anymore. He rolled onto his back and reached up to take hold of the rope hanging from one of the overhead beams. He hoisted himself upright. He grasped his legs and swung them onto the floor, then raised himself off the couch and into his cart. Seated, he could see out the office window: mist heavy in the mill yard and among the trees in the woods, but stirring, lightening, burning off.

Whizzer got his cart pivoted toward the door to the head. He switched on the motor, which started with a hum. Whizzer touched the throttle.

"Giddap," he said.

The mill's proper name was the Dead River Chair Company. It sat on the edge of the village, above the brook that had once driven its changing array of machinery. An old wooden sign on the road side of the mill said DEAD RIVER CHAIR CO. in faded gold letters a foot high. At any time in the past fifty years, however, if you had shown up at the mill looking to buy a chair, the people there would have laughed at you.

There had been a mill on that lot since before the Civil War. At one time and another, it had made about everything you can make out of the kinds of trees that grow in the Vermont foothills: not only chairs, but barrels and tubs, bowls, bobbins, window sash, shutters, boxes, children's sleds, hockey sticks, baskets, gunstocks. The whole outfit had burned to the ground twice, to be rebuilt and refitted finally, around 1910, as the chair company, running out of a big new building with equipment driven, no longer by the brook, but by a steam engine.

The chair company had been owned by three generations of a family named Boot. For sixty years it was a thriving concern. Around the time of the First World War it employed forty people. Leaving out the time needed to season the wood, the mill in its prime could take a log of ash or oak, a log of rock maple, in at one end and pop it out at the other a couple of days later as a full set of good Windsor chairs.

The mill continued to make chairs through the time of Whizzer Boot's grandfather and father, but by the time Whizzer himself took over, it was a diminished thing. Apparently they made a better Windsor chair in North Carolina, in Taiwan, than they did in Vermont. Whizzer nearly went bust. He sold off such of the mill's machinery as he could and left the rest of it to gather cobwebs and bat droppings. He kept up the sawmill, but he moved it out of the mill building and into a metal hangar in the old mill yard. The new sawmill had power not from the chair company's vast and temperamental boiler, but from a diesel engine the size of a TV that could run all week on a barrel of fuel while you drank beer and watched. Whizzer cut and sawed the logs himself until he had his accident. After the accident, he ascended to the level of management.

By and by the mill, which had at times given employment to a whole village, reached the point where it gave employment only to

Whizzer and a couple of helpers. At least, that was the payroll. In fact, nobody at the mill was killing himself with overwork.

Whizzer's accident, now ten years ago, had taken things from him, and it had given him things. The things taken were in the past; they were the past itself. The others continued. The accident had given Whizzer a new way of getting around, a new income, a new job. It had given him a new name. During his long recovery, when he was learning to use the new electric cart or wheelchair in which he was invited to spend the rest of his life, he and the men who idled about the mill, the beer passing among them, would take turns trying the machine out — ahead, back, port, starboard, half speed, full speed. They called the chair the whizzer, and eventually the name of the conveyance attached itself to the conveyed.

Whizzer's accident had also given him his life's only ride in an aircraft, though of that ride he had no memory whatsoever. In fact he had no memory of any part of the event. He had been skidding logs on Little Blue Mountain and had stopped the skidder, set the brake, and gotten down to take a piss. He woke up in the emergency room with a circle of people looking down at him under a bright light. None of them was anybody he knew. He tried to ask them where he was and what had happened to him, but he couldn't seem to make them hear him.

A tree had fallen on him, an oak. They had been cutting oak. The wind had taken the top of an oak being felled; it had twisted off its stump and come down in the wrong place. It had come down on top of Whizzer. Oak's a heavy tree. One that size weighs, maybe, a couple of tons. The oak had hit Whizzer so hard that, as

Coop or D.B. or one of the others said, for five years after the accident he shat mostly acorns.

They got the tree off him, got him out of the woods and down to somebody's pasture, where a helicopter picked him up and took him to the hospital. It took him to the Dartmouth-Hitchcock hospital in New Hampshire. Several days later, when Whizzer understood where he was, he decided he was a gone man in more ways than one. For all that district, Dartmouth-Hitchcock was confidently known to be a waiting room for the Hereafter — or, not a waiting room only, but an export office, a kind of customhouse, where, as you took your departure, whatever you might have had in the way of an earthly estate was distributed without remainder among various members of the medical community.

"Dead or bankrupt," Whizzer said. "Or both."

But, no. Not at all. Ten years later he was alive and more or less solvent, collecting a full disability benefit earned the hard way, and enjoying the attention, the regard, the tender care of a small company of loyal friends whom he could no longer outrun.

Inside, the mill was a long, shadowy hall, poorly lit by filthy windows, where your footfalls on the wooden floorboards were louder than you wished. To either side of a central aisle the old benches, lathes, band saws, jointers, planers, and the rest sat in their dust, and overhead, cables, trolleys, belts, and wheels hung in the gloom. Only at the far end of the floor was there any real light, in the old manager's office, where Whizzer held forth.

The office was a room ten feet square with a window looking out over the mill yard and the brook to the wooded hill beyond them and another window looking onto the mill floor. In the office was a cast-iron woodstove, Whizzer's old leather couch much cracked and scuffed, two steel filing cabinets, packed to overflowing with useless and forgotten paperwork, and half a dozen chairs: rockers, canvas camp chairs, stuffed chairs.

Whizzer had never married, and the mill office, his domain, was neither bright, nor neat, nor clean. On the walls of the office, piled in its corners and on its shelves, stacked atop its cabinets, was an accumulation of the kind of cobwebbed mementos that generations of unsentimental men had hesitated to take to the dump. There were nailed boots and old harness buckles, there were rusty axes and long crosscut saws, also rusty. There were loose bars, sprockets, carburetors from chain-saw engines. There were brown photographs, framed, showing groups of men with suspenders and heavy mustaches standing in front of piles of enormous logs, the mill behind them.

High on one wall loomed the head and antlers of a great caribou. Whizzer's late father had been a big-game hunter. He had brought the caribou trophy back from Alaska, where in 1948 he had been led into the Brooks Range by the great Elwood "Grizzly" Singleton, dean of Alaskan big game guides. The senior Boot had drawn a blank in the game department out there. In two miserable weeks neither he nor Singleton had so much as fired his rifle. The caribou had come from a taxidermist's shop in Vancouver. As Whizzer's father told the story, Grizzly Singleton had insisted on buying the head as a present to him before the disappointed hunter boarded the Canadian Pacific for the long haul back to New England. Singleton's client had been promised a mount, and the Grizzly was an honorable man though, as was well known to every sportsman from San Francisco to Fairbanks, a lousy guide.

Another trophy in Whizzer's office was his own: a great horned owl, which glared with its angry glass eyes from a shelf behind the door. It had turned up dead in the mill yard one morning long ago, and Whizzer, then a high school kid, had determined to stuff it. He found instructions in a boys' magazine. He skinned the bird and had one of the men at the mill shape a kind of wooden football to fit inside it more or less, then he packed sawdust into the empty spaces, sewed the whole thing up, and wired it onto a branch nailed to a board. The glass eyes he mail-ordered from Chicago. They were the most satisfactory part of the exhibit — or the least unsatisfactory. Apart from the eyes, Whizzer's owl hadn't held up well. It looked like it ought, in the first place, to have been given a decent burial. It had developed a drunken lean to one side, and over the years mice had moved into its interior and nested there. When they frolicked, the stuffed owl could sometimes be seen faintly to jerk or twitch, as if in life. Some days, indeed, Whizzer's owl got around the premises more than Whizzer.

Closing in on a hundred years old, built entirely of wooden timbers, studs, boards, and shingles, all of which were saturated with ancient grease, the mill amounted to a large firework waiting for a match. Whizzer couldn't afford to insure it. The property existed on the town's grand list like a crazy aunt in the attic, a painful embarrassment never to be discussed. At any time in the past fifteen years, the town might have seized the place for unpaid taxes, but they didn't. Why would they? They didn't want the mill. Nobody wanted it. It wasn't worth demolishing. It wasn't worth thinking about. One day, it would burn down.

Until that day Whizzer kept his little sawmill going off and on in the yard beside the old chair company building, and he kept a kind of club in the office. There was a coffeepot, and there was a cooler. There was the stove for winter and an electric fan for summer. In there, Whizzer sat with whoever turned up: men bringing logs to the mill, the kids he had helping him in the yard, passersby, and a fairly constant set of three or four men a little younger than he, who came and went. They sat in the office and talked — or didn't. They watched the ball games on a little TV Whizzer had set up. If a quantity of beer should make itself available, they drank it. The time passed. The mill was no Mermaid Tavern, no, but it did what it had to do in its time. And anyway, how many Mermaid Taverns do you need?

3

YOU PEOPLE

Somebody drove into the yard.

"Who's this?" asked Whizzer.

Coop got to his feet and went to the window. He looked out.

"Lady in a little car," said Coop.

"Young?" Whizzer asked.

Coop bent to the window.

"I wouldn't call it young," he said. "It's a 'ninety-two, 'ninety-three. A little Escort."

"The lady," said Whizzer.

Coop looked again.

"Young enough," he said.

"Well, tell her to bring a couple of friends, then," said Whizzer. "We've got a party going in here, tell her."

"You tell her," said Coop.

"Who is she?" D.B. asked him.

"Don't know her name," said Coop. "Used to work at Edie's."

"What's Edie's?" asked Conrad.

There were four of them in the office. They waited for the newcomer to park her car. They heard her slam the door, then they heard her steps echo on the mill floor. Then she was with them.

"Morning," said Whizzer. The young woman stood in the door of the office. She looked from one of the men to the others.

"Which one is Whizzer?" she said.

Whizzer raised his hand.

"You know Scott?" the young woman asked him. "Scott Cavanaugh?"

"Scotty?" Whizzer said. "Sure. Sure, we do."

"I'm looking for him," the young woman said. "Is he around?"

"You're looking for Scotty?" Whizzer asked.

"I was told I'd find him here," the young woman said.

"Who told you that?" Coop asked her.

The young woman didn't reply to him. She spoke to Whizzer.

"The sheriff told me," she said.

"Wingate?" Coop said.

"He said I could get help here, from Scott Cavanaugh."

"Well, Scotty ain't here," said Coop.

"He's upstate," said D.B. "He went to White River."

"Visits his brother up there," said Coop.

"It ain't his brother, it's his uncle," said D.B. "The one whose kid's been in the hospital. That's Scotty's uncle."

"What's the matter with the kid?" asked Conrad.

"Look . . . ," began the young woman.

"I thought it was his brother," said Coop.

"Well, it ain't," said D.B.

"Leukemia," said Whizzer.

"Oh, boy," said Conrad.

"He'll be back this afternoon late," said Whizzer to the young woman. "Scotty. He'll probably stop by then."

"This afternoon?" the young woman said.

"What do you want with Scotty?" Whizzer asked her.

"I need his help," the young woman said.

"You're Russell's boy's girl, ain't you?" D.B. asked her. "You're Kevin's girl."

"I was," said the young woman.

"You're the girl turned Blackway in," Coop said.

"That's why she's looking for help," said D.B. "Ain't it?" he asked the young woman.

"That's why," said the young woman.

The three men shut up and looked at Whizzer. Whizzer was sitting in his cart. He hitched himself up in the seat. He spoke to the young woman.

"What kind of help did you want from Scotty?" he asked.

"What's Blackway doing to you?" Coop asked.

"He's following me. I told the sheriff."

"Blackway's following you?" Whizzer asked her.

"He's watching me," the young woman said. "He trashed my car. He killed my cat."

"Blackway killed your cat?" D.B. asked her.

"He wants to hurt me," the young woman said. "The sheriff knows. He killed Annabelle because she was mine. To show me. What he would do. What he could do anytime he wanted to. I went to the sheriff. I told the sheriff: He won't stop there. He knows Blackway. He told me there's nothing he can do. He told me to find Cavanaugh. He told me to come to you. I came. What am I going to do?"

"Get another cat?" said D.B.

"There you go," said Coop.

"Leave town?" said D.B.

"Leave town?" the young woman asked. "You mean run away?"

"There you go," said Coop.

The young woman shook her head. She spoke to Whizzer. "No," she said. "I won't do that. I'm here. I'm staying. I told the sheriff. I didn't do anything wrong. I will not run. Let Blackway run."

"Pistol, ain't you?" D.B. said.

"Come to that," said Coop, "she's right. Why should she run? Blackway'd just go looking for her."

"Find her, too," said D.B.

"What do you want Scotty to do for you?" Whizzer asked the young woman.

"The sheriff said he could help me," she said. "He could do something. Go with me, because of Blackway. He could go with me."

Whizzer looked across the little room to D.B. and Coop. He looked back at the young woman.

"He could, I guess," Whizzer said. "But he ain't here."

The young woman nodded. She looked around at the three men sitting before her on chairs or on the desk, and at Whizzer in his cart.

"That's it, then?" she asked.

"I guess it is, about," said Whizzer.

"You guess it is?" the young woman said. "What's the matter with you people?"

"You people?" Whizzer said.

"All of you," the young woman said. "The sheriff. You. What's wrong with you? I come to you for help. I've got no place else to go. The sheriff gives me a speech about the law. Your friend isn't around. And you guess that's it?"

"Take it easy, now," said Whizzer.

"Don't tell me to take it easy."

"Take it easy," said Coop.

"Fuck you," the young woman said. She turned and started for the door.

"Take it easy," said D.B.

"What about Nate the Great?" Coop asked.

"Nate?" Whizzer said. The young woman paused in the doorway.

"Sure," Coop said. "She needs somebody to go with her. Nate would do it. He'd go with her, you asked him to."

"He's a kid," said Whizzer.

"Wait a minute," said the young woman.

"He's a big kid," said Coop.

"That's so," said Whizzer. To the young woman he said, "Hang on." To D.B. he said, "Get him in here."

"Wait a minute," said the young woman.

Nate the Great was around back. He was working with Lester — old Lester Speed. They were unloading cement blocks from Whizzer's flatbed. They had the truck backed up over the bank, above. Lester was up on the bed with the blocks, and Nate was down the bank, eight or ten feet below, where the blocks were to end up. Lester wanted to push the blocks off the truck and let them fall and land on the ground where Nate could pick them up and move them to a pile behind him. Nate wanted Lester to drop the blocks so he could catch them before they landed. Each block weighed thirty pounds.

"Come on," said Nate.

"Get back," Lester said. But Nate had been after him since they had started, so he shoved a block off the truck with Nate directly below. Nate caught the block two-handed, like a basketball, set it down, and called for another. That one he caught one-handed. Soon they had a rhythm going between them, but still Lester didn't like it.

"That's enough," he said. "Get back, now."

"Come on," said Nate.

"We had a young fellow like you in the woods," Lester said. "Showboat. He liked to catch butts off the loader. Hundred, hundred and fifty pounds, one of them would weigh. Oak butts. He caught them like they were made of — I don't know — shaving foam. Like they were made of feathers. Do it all day long."

"Come on," said Nate.

"Until one day, I guess he wasn't paying attention," Lester went on. "Thinking about his girlfriend, probably. Came a butt. He didn't see it. Knocked him down, broke his neck."

"I ain't got a girlfriend," Nate said. "Come on."

"Killed him," said Lester. "Killed him right there."

D.B. came around the truck and stood on the top of the bank.

"Nate?" he said.

"Yo," said Nate.

"Boss wants you."

"Yo," said Nate. He climbed up the bank. D.B. had turned back to the mill. Nate followed him. A tall, long-boned, heavy-wristed kid: not a scholar, not a talker. Smarter than a horse, not smarter than a tractor.

Nate followed D.B. into the office and waited in the doorway beside the young woman. Tall as she was, the top of her head was two inches below Nate's shoulder.

"You about done out there?" Whizzer asked Nate.

"About," said Nate.

"This lady needs you to go with her to find Blackway," Whizzer said.

"Wait a minute," the young woman said. "Who's he?"

"This is Nate the Great," said Coop.

"Helps out around the yard," said D.B.

"A hired man?" the young woman asked. "Hired boy? You're giving me a hired boy to go with me? What about Blackway?"

"Blackway's been interfering with her," Whizzer told Nate.

"Been following her around," said Coop.

"Been stalking her, like," said D.B.

"Smashed her car," said Coop.

"Wait a minute," said the young woman.

"Killed her cat," said Coop.

"Killed her cat?" said Nate.

"Look," said the young woman. "Forget it, all right? I came here for What's-his-name — Cavanaugh. He's not here. Fine. That's my problem, not yours. I don't want the hired help. Let's just forget the whole thing."

Whizzer ignored her. "You willing to go with her?" he asked Nate.

"I don't mind," Nate said.

"You know Blackway?" Whizzer asked him.

"Seen him."

"You think you can handle him?" Coop asked.

"I guess," said Nate.

"What makes you think so?" Whizzer asked.

"He's old, ain't he?"

Whizzer looked around at the other men.

"He might be forty," Whizzer said.

"Nate the Great here will help you out," D.B. told the young woman.

"He will not," said the young woman. "I told you: I don't want him. This kid belongs at basketball practice."

"You belong at basketball practice?" Whizzer asked Nate.

Nate shrugged.

Whizzer turned to the young woman. "Ma'am," he said, "I don't see you've got a lot of choice here. Do you? You went to the sheriff. You didn't like what he told you. You came here for Scotty. Scotty ain't to be had. You're scared of Blackway. So's everybody else. If you had any sense, you'd leave town. You won't do that. You don't think you should have to. Maybe you're right. 'Course you are. But I don't quite see your next move, is the thing. Do you? I guess you could go to Blackway on your own, treat him nice, ask him nice to let up on you."

"Appeal to his better nature," said Coop.

"Get down on your knees," said D.B.

"There you go," said Coop.

"It might work," said D.B.

"Fuck you," said the young woman.

"You said that before," Whizzer said.

"I know what I said," said the young woman. "Do you want me to say it again? Okay. Fuck you." But she didn't move to leave the room.

"Well, then," said Whizzer. To Nate he said, "You might's well get started, if you're ready."

"You want us to finish with the blocks first?" Nate asked him.

"No, go ahead," Whizzer said.

"Where to?" Nate asked.

Whizzer looked at D.B. D.B. shook his head.

"Blackway's got a camp in the Towns," Coop said. "Had it for years. I don't know just where, though."

"What Towns?" Conrad asked.

"The Empty Towns," said Coop.

"Lost Towns, we used to call them," said D.B.

"You been to the Towns?" Whizzer asked the young woman.

"No," she said.

"You been there?" Whizzer asked Nate. "Know your way around up there, at all?"

"No," said Nate. "Never been in there."

"Les has," Coop said. "Les used to work logging up there. He worked there for years. He knows the Towns as well as Blackway, better. Send Les with them."

"Who's Les?" the young woman asked.

Whizzer nodded toward the doorway. Lester was there, behind her. Where had he come from? He hadn't come in with Nate. Lester had simply appeared in the doorway.

"You been hearing this?" Whizzer asked Lester.

"Sure," said Lester.

"You know the country up there?"

"Oh, sure," said Lester. "I've been all through there, working, hunting. 'Course, that was some time ago. But I can find my way, I expect."

The young woman had been looking at Lester as he answered. "Some time ago?" she said. "How much time? A hundred years? You're sending me after Blackway with the kid who does the chores and somebody out of the old folks' home?"

Again Whizzer ignored her. "You want to go along with them?" he asked Lester. "Help them find Blackway?"

"You mean now?" Lester asked.

Whizzer nodded.

"Sure," Lester said.

"Can we just forget the whole thing?" the young woman asked. "Let's just forget it."

"Blackway might take some finding, you know," Coop said to Lester. "You'll have to look here and there — you know where."

"I know," said Lester.

"You want to go by the High Line," said Coop.

"What High Line?" asked Conrad.

"I know," said Lester.

"Wait," said the young woman. "Just wait a minute."

"You want to try the Fort," said D.B.

"What Fort?" asked Conrad.

"I know," said Lester.

"Before you go out up into the puckerbrush," said Coop, "into the Towns."

"I know," said Lester.

"Plus," Whizzer said, "Blackway ain't alone. There's going to be others."

"Friends of Blackway's," said Coop.

"I know," said Lester.

"I told you, I don't want —" the young woman began.

"Fitz has been working with Blackway," Whizzer told Lester.

"I heard that," said Coop.

"He might know where Blackway is," said Whizzer. "I'd go see Fitz."

"We'll do that," said Lester.

"You got everything you need in the way of — you know?" Whizzer asked him.

"We'll get it," said Lester.

"All right, then," said Whizzer. To the young woman he said,

"You take these fellows along with you, now. Go ahead. They'll help you with Blackway. And if they don't, you can always cuss him to death."

D.B. laughed, but the young woman wasn't happy.

"It's not just me, you know," she said. "It's them. They have no chance. Blackway will eat them alive."

"Maybe not," said Whizzer.

The young woman shook her head. "You'll see," she said. She turned and pushed her way out of the office past Nate and Lester. Nate followed her. Lester turned to go.

"Les?" Whizzer said.

Lester turned back to the office.

"Keep your eye on him," said Whizzer. "Look out for him. Nate the Great. He's apt to get into stuff and not think. He don't always think. He don't know how."

"Sure," said Lester.

"You really got everything you need?" Whizzer asked him.

"Sure."

"Because," Whizzer went on, "you know, if you get in there, you get close, you can't go back. You got to be ready to go all the way through."

"Sure."

"Okay, then," said Whizzer.

Lester left the office to go after the young woman and Nate. Whizzer and the others heard their footfalls on the mill floor, then they didn't. Coop got up and went to the window.

"They're taking Nate the Great's truck," he said.

"Girl's a piece of work, ain't she?" said D.B.

"Who is she?" Conrad asked.

"Hair down to her ass," said Coop. "See her hair?"

"Thinks she's a cut above, too, don't she?" said D.B. "*What's the matter with you people?*"

"Whiz liked her all right," said Coop.

"Did you?" Conrad asked Whizzer.

"Sure," said Whizzer.

"Whiz likes hair," said Coop.

"Wishes he had more of his own," said D.B.

"What's the matter with her hair?" Whizzer asked.

"*You people?*" said D.B. "Cat named Annabelle? Thinks she's something. Thinks she's — what do you call that?"

"You call that attitude," said Conrad.

"Attitude on her," said D.B. "Who's she think she is, anyway?"

"Who is she, really?" asked Conrad. "Is she local?"

"No," said Coop. "She's not from here. From the city, it looks like."

"The city?" said Whizzer. "No, she ain't. Not a chance. She's no city girl. She ain't from right here, maybe, but she didn't come far to get here."

"How do you know that?" Conrad asked him.

"Whiz can spot a woodchuck a mile off," said D.B.

"Takes one to know one," said Whizzer.

"Wherever she's from, she's some little pistol, there, ain't she?" said D.B. "*She* won't run from Blackway. Hell, no."

"She's right," said Whizzer. "She ain't done nothing. No reason she should run. Would you?"

"Run from Blackway?" D.B. answered. "Hell, yes."

Coop went to the coffeepot. "Mouth on her, too," he said. "Did you hear her? Fuck this, fuck that. I thought I was back in the navy."

"I know it," said D.B. "One thing, though: Girls that talk like that? They put out."

"How would you know?" Coop asked him. "You never knew a girl that talked like that before."

"He never knew a girl that put out before, either," said Whizzer.

"Don't you mind about what girls I knew," said D.B.

"Same ones I did, it looks like," said Coop.

"She's right about Les and Nate the Great, though," said D.B. "They can't go up against Blackway."

"Can't they?' asked Whizzer.

"Who's Blackway?" asked Conrad.

"Who's Blackway?" Coop said. "Who's Blackway, Whiz?"

"I don't quite know what to tell you," said Whizzer. "Blackway's a local fellow."

"Blackway's a fellow you don't want to fool with," said D.B.

"Blackway's bad news," said Coop.

"What do you mean?" asked Conrad. "What does he do?"

"Do?" asked Whizzer. "Well, how would you put it? Blackway's kind of an entrepreneur."

"An entrepreneur?" Coop said.

"Whatever he is," said D.B., "I wouldn't want Blackway following me around. I know that."

"You're in no danger," said Coop. "What Blackway wants, you ain't got."

"What does he want?" Conrad asked them.

"What does he want?" said D.B. "You mean from her? Come on. You're a married man. Do we have to draw you a picture, here? You know what he wants. So does What's-her-name."

"What is her name?" Conrad asked.

"I knew," said Coop. "Can't recall. Susie?"

"Sally?" said D.B.

"Lillian," said Whizzer. "Her name is Lillian. And that ain't either what Blackway wants with her."

"What, then?" Conrad asked.

"To teach her a lesson," said Whizzer.

"What lesson?" Conrad asked him. "Why?"

"Because she got him fired," said Whizzer.

"Fouled up his game," said Coop.

"What game?" Conrad asked.

Conrad was married to Whizzer's younger sister. He was a smart man, but he was a man who didn't know the ground. He didn't know the ground, and he thought you could learn the ground by asking questions. A man of questions, a man from away. "What game?" Conrad asked.

"That thing with the dope," Coop said.

"What dope?" Conrad asked.

"That thing with Russell's kid," said Whizzer.

"What kid?" Conrad asked.

4

BLACKWAY'S VISIT

"What a bunch of clowns," said Lillian.

"Can't hear you," said Lester.

They were bouncing around in Nate's truck on their way to Fitzgerald's. The motor roared, and the gears screamed, and the tailgate, which was wired shut, rattled and banged.

"I said, what a bunch of clowns."

"Who?"

Nate drove, with Lester on the outside and Lillian in the middle, between them.

"Back there," said Lillian.

"You mean Whizzer and them?"

"Idiots."

"They ain't idiots," said Lester.

"What would you call them?" asked Lillian.

"I wouldn't call them idiots," said Lester. "Not exactly."

"No?" said Lillian. "What are they, then? What do they do in there?"

"They get the news. Keep track of things."

"No, they don't. Look, I know all about them. Guys like that. You think I don't? I do. I know them too well. I know everything about them. They do nothing. They sit there. All day, every day, they sit in there. That's what they do: nothing."

"They talk things over," said Lester.

"They talk, all right," said Lillian. "You're right about that. They talk. They talk to themselves. If you knew how sick I am of talk."

"Everybody talks," said Lester.

"Not like them. Clowns. Nine o'clock in the morning? I bet they were half in the bag — all of them."

"You mean drunk?"

"Something," said Lillian. "They weren't stoned. They're too old. But they were doing something. They had to be. Listen to them. They sound like a flock of chickens, the way they talk. Nobody who isn't doing something talks like that."

"Like what?" asked Lester.

Fitzgerald lived a few miles out of town in a big house that had a view of the mountains to the west, which, as the fog broke up, showed themselves in the morning sunlight, far off, a pale blue limit. Fitzgerald had had the place built ten years before, out of redwood, shingles, stone, and glass. He'd had it built low, all on one floor, like a new house ought to be. He'd spent a lot of money. Fitzgerald did pretty well. He was the biggest logger in that part of the state, he had a couple of dozen men working for him. Maybe he wasn't a genius, but he was honest and fair, he'd been lucky and he'd worked hard, and he'd done pretty well for himself. Until now.

They found the house shut up tight with the blinds down and no lights showing.

"Nobody's here," said Lillian.

"Don't look as though there is, does it?" Lester said.

He got down from the truck and went to the front door. He tried the knob and found the door locked. He rang the bell. No response. Inside the house, a dog began to bark, not a big dog, by the sound, but a little, yapping dog. Lester began knocking on the door, and as he did he began calling, "Fred? Fred? Come on, Fred."

The door opened a foot and Fitzgerald peered out. He looked

like hell: no shave, skin gray, eyes red, clothes slept-in, breath like an empty bottle in which a mouse has died.

"Les?" said Fitzgerald.

"Morning," Lester said. "We see you for a minute?"

"We?" Fitzgerald said.

Lester beckoned toward the truck, and Nate and Lillian got out and came to the house to stand with Lester. Fitzgerald watched them unhappily from the doorway.

"Who's she?" he asked Lester.

"Blackway's been making trouble for her," said Lester. "We're trying to get it sorted out."

"Blackway?" said Fitzgerald. He stepped back from the doorway and tried to shut the door against them, but Lester put out his hand and held it.

"Fred?" he asked.

"Oh," Fitzgerald said. "Sure." He stepped back and let them into the house. A little brown dog, some kind of terrier, yapped at them from behind Fitzgerald's legs as they entered.

"Shut up," Fitzgerald told the dog. He closed the door and turned the lock. Then he rattled the door to make sure it was tight.

"I'm a little under the weather, here," said Fitzgerald.

"I can see," said Lester.

"Been up all night," said Fitzgerald.

Lester nodded.

"Night before, too," said Fitzgerald. "Truth is, I've been pretty shitfaced. Cynthia doesn't like me to start drinking in the morning."

"How is Cynthia?"

"Like me. Worse. She took a sleeping pill. Went to bed."

"You ought to do the same."

"Can't," said Fitzgerald.

"What about Heidi?" Lester asked him. "Where's she?"

"She's at school," said Fitzgerald. "She doesn't know."

"Know what?"

"You want coffee?" Fitzgerald asked them.

"No," said Lillian. Nate shook his head.

"Sure," said Lester.

"Come on," Fitzgerald said. He turned and wobbled ahead of them toward the kitchen. When the others started after him, Fitzgerald's dog began barking at them all over again.

"Shut up," Fitzgerald told the dog.

In the kitchen Fitzgerald waved them toward a round table with four chairs. On the table were two or three dirty glasses and a half-empty bottle of Jim Beam. On the table as well lay a big Colt revolver, loaded.

Lester took a chair and sat at the table where he could watch Fitzgerald. Nate and Lillian remained standing. Lester looked at the revolver on the table. With his forefinger he gently pushed its barrel around so it pointed off to the side.

"What's this for, Fred?" Lester asked Fitzgerald.

"I've been sitting out here," Fitzgerald said. He was at the stove. He made two cups of instant coffee and carried them, one at a time, to the table. He sat across from Lester and picked up the bottle. He held the bottle over Lester's coffee cup, waiting.

"Sure," said Lester.

Fitzgerald poured whiskey into Lester's coffee, then into his own. He set the bottle down.

"What's this for?" Lester asked again.

Fitzgerald drank from his cup.

"How do you mean?" he asked.

"Come on, Fred."

Fitzgerald's little dog seemed to have taken against Lillian, who stood behind Lester's chair. The dog began yapping at her. Lillian knelt and held out her hand for the dog to approach, but it backed away from her and kept on yapping.

"Shut up," Fitzgerald told the dog.

"We're looking for Blackway," Lester said.

"Then you're drunker than I am," said Fitzgerald.

"Fred?"

"He was here," said Fitzgerald. He looked at the revolver on the table. "That was my uncle Joe's," he said. "He was a game warden. You remember him?"

"Sure," said Lester.

"He carried it," Fitzgerald went on. "The shells were his, too. Joe's been dead for twenty years. I don't even know if they'd fire anymore."

"What happened with Blackway?" Lester asked him.

"I saw Joe fire it once when I was a little kid," Fitzgerald said. "He couldn't get it to hit a god damned thing."

"What happened, Fred?"

"Makes a pretty good bang, though," Fitzgerald said.

"Fred?"

"Listen," said Fitzgerald. "Blackway and I weren't ever friends or anything. It was a business thing. Blackway knows a lot of people: people that have money, people that want money. Say maybe he knew somebody who had some woods, wanted to raise some cash. Blackway would talk to the owner. He'd make the contract. Then we'd go in and do the cut, Blackway gets a fee. That was all. Maybe once, twice a year, Blackway would come in with a job for us. He was like an agent. Once or twice a year. Not that often."

"Sure," said Lester.

"So, late April, May," Fitzgerald said, "Blackway comes in with a job on a big lot in Jamaica. Owner's not around, he's here summers, lives in — I don't know — Boston. But Blackway's got his signed contract: so many feet, bounds, roads, you know how it works. It was two hundred acres, all on the side of the mountain, over there. Looks okay, so off we go."

Lillian took the chair beside Lester and sat. When she did, the little dog jumped up from its place on the floor by Fitzgerald's feet and began yapping at her again.

"Shut up," Fitzgerald told the dog.

"We've been in there I guess six weeks," he went on. "Monday morning, I get a call at the office from George, the job boss. Seems he's had a visit from a Mr. Simmons and a sheriff's deputy. Those are Simmons's woods we're cutting. Simmons is the owner. He is pissed. He wonders what the hell is going on here. He doesn't know anything about any logging job. He doesn't know anything about any contract. What he does know is he's got about forty acres less woods than he thought he had. Seems he's headed to the office with the deputy."

"Some mistake," said Lester.

"What I thought," said Fitzgerald. "I wasn't too worried. It had to be some kind of confusion, didn't it? Because, after all, I had the contract, Blackway's contract. It was a done deal."

"Sure," said Lester.

"So Mr. Simmons and the deputy turn up. He's hot, yes, he is.

He's one of these rich guys, owns his own mountain, thinks every tree on it is his pet tree. The deputy? The deputy acts like he's having trouble keeping awake, the way they all do. I bring out my contract, show it to Simmons. Simmons says he never saw it before in his life, never signed any such paper, never heard of Blackway, never talked about logging those woods with him or anybody else. His signature on the contract? Forged. And what am I going to do about his trees?"

"Blackway forged the owner's name on the paper?" Lester asked.

"Somebody did," said Fitzgerald. "That was Monday. Of course, I tried to reach Blackway. Of course, I couldn't. Mr. Simmons says I'll be hearing from his lawyer. I expect I will, too. I don't have a lawyer. Deputy told me to go to Ripley Wingate."

"Wingate," said Lester. He looked at Lillian. Lillian raised her eyebrows at him, but said nothing.

"That was Monday, like I said," Fitzgerald went on. "I was going to see Wingate the next day. That night, middle of the night, Cynthia and I are in bed, sound asleep. I wake up. For a minute I don't know why — then I do. Somebody's sitting on the edge of the bed, our bed, just sitting there in the dark. I feel his weight on the bed, and it wakes me up. Now I can see him, kind of, in the moonlight coming in the window, his shadow. I reach for the light.

"'Leave it off,' he says. It's Blackway.

"Cynthia's awake, too. 'Who is it? Who's there?' she's saying, but I shush her. Blackway pays her no attention. He's talking to me, low, not whispering, but talking low.

"'You saw that owner.'

"'That's right.'

"'What are you going to do?'

"'I don't know.'

"'I heard you were going to talk to Wingate.'

"'I thought about it.'

"'You don't want to do that,' Blackway says.

"'Heidi,' Cynthia says. 'Where's Heidi?' Heidi's room's down the hall from ours. 'Where's Heidi?' Cynthia's crying. I shush her.

"'You don't want to take this any farther,' Blackway says. 'You see that, don't you?'

"'Yes,' I say.

"'Where's my daughter?' Cynthia says. 'Where's Heidi?'

"'Here,' Blackway says. He hands something to her. It's Heidi's bear, her doll, like a toy she sleeps with. Blackway has it. He gives it to Cynthia.

"'You see what you're into, here, don't you?' Blackway asks me.

"'Yes,' I say.

"'You going to talk to Wingate now?'

"'No,' I say.

"'Good,' Blackway says. He gets up off the bed and stands beside it.

"Cynthia's crying. Blackway doesn't say anything. He's standing there looking down at us. I see him turn in the moonlight, or maybe it's his shadow on the wall, I don't know, and then he's gone. Cynthia gets up and goes to Heidi's room. She's asleep. Cynthia comes back to bed. We just lie there the rest of the night. We don't talk, just lie there. That was Monday night — Tuesday morning. Today is — what?"

"Wednesday," said Lester.

"Wednesday," said Fitzgerald.

"You didn't go to Wingate, then?" Lester asked him.

"Are you serious?" Fitzgerald said.

"'Course, the deputy knows all about this," said Lester.

"I can't help that," said Fitzgerald. "All I can do is shut up. That's what he told me to do. That's what I'm doing."

"Sure," said Lester.

"What I don't see," Fitzgerald said, "is how he ever thought he'd get away with just signing the guy's name and having us go ahead with the job. How did he think he was going to get away with that?"

"He didn't," said Lester.

"He didn't?"

"No," said Lester. "He didn't care about getting away with anything. He didn't care about people finding out. He wanted them to find out. He cared about making trouble. Trouble is what Blackway's after."

"He came in here," said Fitzgerald. "When we were sleeping. He was on our bed. He was in our little girl's room."

"You were lucky," said Lillian.

"Lucky?" said Fitzgerald. "I was lucky?"

"Take it easy, Fred," said Lester. "He's gone."

"What if he comes back?"

"What if he does?" asked Lester. He nodded at the revolver that lay before them on the table. "You going to shoot him?"

"No," said Fitzgerald. "I got it out. I don't know why. Cynthia's scareder of it than she is of Blackway."

"Put it away, Fred," said Lester.

"Okay," said Fitzgerald.

"You know where he is?" Lester asked Fitzgerald.

"Blackway? God, no. Why ask me?"

"Well," said Lester. "If we're going to do anything about him, we've got to find him. If we're going to find him, we've got to start somewhere. We're starting with you."

"What for?" Fitzgerald asked him. "What do you want with Blackway?"

"Nothing," said Lester. "It's her." He nodded at Lillian.

"What's she want with Blackway?"

"Wants him to go away," said Lester. "Ain't that about it?" he asked Lillian. Lillian nodded.

"To go away?" Fitzgerald asked.

"Blackway's been tailing her around," said Lester. "Threatening her. Like."

"Busted up her car," said Nate.

"Killed her cat," said Lester.

"He killed her cat?" Fitzgerald asked. "Jesus, why does she wait? Why doesn't she take off? Get out of here?"

"Don't want to, it looks like," said Lester. "Don't see why she should."

"Why she should?" Fitzgerald said. "Jesus. How much more reason does she need?"

"Pistol, this one is," said Lester.

"Jesus," said Fitzgerald again. He reached for the bottle. "You want another one?" he asked Lester.

"Where would you go to find Blackway?" Lester asked him.

"No place," said Fitzgerald. "I told you: I've seen enough of Blackway."

"Fred?"

"You might try over on Diamond," Fitzgerald said. "There's a crew just getting done over there. They're all in with Blackway. If he's not there, they'll know where he is."

"Okay, then," said Lester.

He rose from his chair. Lillian did the same. Nate had remained standing. When Lillian stood, Fitzgerald's dog began barking again. Fitzgerald sat at his table, staring at the bottle, at the revolver. He looked like he'd forgotten where he was. His dog yapped and yapped.

"Shut up," Fitzgerald told the dog.

5

THE ARGUMENT

Nate slammed the truck's door. He started the engine and looked at Lester.

"We'll swing by my place," said Lester.

"Wait a minute," said Lillian. "I thought we were going after Blackway."

"We are," said Lester. "We'll make a pickup first."

"What pickup?" Lillian asked. Lester said nothing. "What pickup?" she asked Nate.

Nate didn't answer. He turned the truck around in Fitzgerald's yard and started back out his lane to the road.

"Can't he talk?" Lillian asked Lester.

"Don't know," said Lester. "Can you talk?" he asked Nate.

"No," said Nate.

"How I hate a yappy little dog like that thing Fred has," Lester said. "Won't shut up. Good for nothing but noise. Thing is, how did that dog come not to bark at Blackway, I wonder. He barked at us. He barked all the time. He wouldn't shut up. How did he come not to bark and wake Fred up when Blackway broke in the other night?" He looked at Nate.

"Who?" asked Nate.

"The dog."

"Don't know."

"Well," said Lester, "everybody says Blackway's got plenty of moves. Poor Fred, locked up in there drunk as a skunk, with the old warden's forty-four. What did he think?"

"Blackway won't be scared off by a gun," said Lillian.

"I ain't scared of Blackway," said Nate.

"You should be," said Lillian.

"You don't think we're up to Blackway, do you?" Lester asked her. "You ain't got the confidence."

"You could say that," said Lillian.

"Confidence," said Lester. "That's why we're going to swing by my place."

"After that, we go to Blackway?" Lillian asked.

"Well," said Lester, "by and by."

"What does that mean?"

"I ain't worried about Blackway," said Lester, "much as I'm worried about getting to Blackway."

"I thought he's with the loggers," said Lillian. "In the woods. We're going there, right? We'll find him there."

"We might," said Lester. "Likely there'll be a bit more to it than that, though."

"What more?"

"Well," said Lester, "Blackway's got friends."

"Friends?"

"Call them that."

"Look," said Lillian, "I don't want anything to do with any friends of Blackway's."

"You're the one wants us to take care of Blackway, ain't you?" Lester asked her. "To take care of him we got to find him. To find him we got to go through them others."

"What others are you talking about?" Lillian asked him, but nobody answered her. Nate was bringing the truck into the driveway beside Lester's house.

Lester lived in a tiny hamlet called Boyceville. Boyceville was strung out along the road, seven houses and a barn, nothing else: no post office, no school, no store. The settlement had grown up over the years around the old Boyce farm, as sons and daughters, nephews and nieces, had put up their own places. Evidently the Boyces didn't like to travel far. In time they learned, however. They were long gone, except for Elvira Percy, a great-granddaughter of one of the Boyces who'd had the farm. The farm was extinct, the barn falling down. There remained the seven houses. Of them, the last one in the collection before you reached the town line was Lester's.

It was a small bungalow, a flimsy house built on the cheap not quite long enough ago for cheapness to be reliably consistent with quality. Lester and his wife, Irene, had bought it thirty years earlier. He was working in the woods at the time and didn't put in a lot of effort on his own place. Irene and their girls were the ones who kept the house up. Then more recently, when Irene had at last had enough of Lester and had moved to Florida to live with their older girl, Lester had pretty much let the house go. He didn't clean, he didn't paint. He did, however, keep Irene's little picket fence along the road in good repair. And he kept up, and added to, the collection of whirligigs in the front yard.

These were tin and wooden pinwheels — toys, really — set up on poles to turn in the wind, imitating different actions. There was a flying goose, a flying bumblebee, a man chopping wood, a man rowing a boat, an Indian paddling a canoe, a dog with a wagging tail, a running horse. Clever rigs, in their way. Lester had even contrived a whirligig of a man who dropped his trousers to show his pink behind to the passing motorist. Fifteen or twenty whirligigs stood about Lester's yard, flailing and jumping in the wind, clattering. Lester made them in his kitchen with a jigsaw he had set up in there. The whirligigs were for sale, and from time to time some-body bought one, but Lester made the things mainly because Irene and their girls had liked them. He was sentimental about Irene and their girls.

Lester left the truck and went to the door of the house and in. Lillian and Nate sat in the truck and waited for him. After a moment Nate reached forward and turned off the engine.

"I've always wondered who lived here," Lillian said.

Nate didn't say anything.

"Does he have a wife?" Lillian asked him. "A family?"

"Who?" asked Nate.

"Him." Lillian nodded toward the house. "Lester."

"Les? Don't know."

They watched Lester's whirligigs pivoting and jerking about in the yard like a clockwork kindergarten.

"Did he make all these things?" Lillian asked Nate.

"Don't know."

"If he does have a wife, I feel sorry for her," said Lillian. "Look at this place."

Nate didn't respond. They listened to the whirligigs clacking in the wind. After a moment Lillian asked him, "How old is he?"

"Who?"

"Lester, okay? Your partner. Lester. Lester. Who have we been talking about?"

"Les?" said Nate. "Don't know. Pretty old."

"Right," said Lillian. "Look: Tell me the truth. Can he, can you do this, with Blackway? Really do it?"

Nate didn't answer her. He watched the whirligigs. After a couple of minutes he spoke again.

"I ain't scared of Blackway," said Nate.

Lester came out the side door of his place and around to the truck. He had a long parcel wrapped up in a black plastic trash bag under his arm. He opened the truck's door, laid his parcel carefully on the floor behind the seat, and got in beside Lillian.

"What's that?" Lillian asked him.

"Curtain rods," said Lester.

"Curtain rods?" said Lillian. "It's a gun, isn't it? That's some kind of gun."

Nate started the truck's engine and backed it out of Lester's driveway into the road.

"Curtain rods," said Lester.

"Wait a minute," said Lillian. "No guns. Nobody said anything about guns. I don't want any guns in this."

"Hold it," Lester said to Nate.

Nate stopped the truck.

"Turn it off," said Lester. Nate shut off the engine. They were stopped in the middle of the road. Lester turned to Lillian.

"Okay," he said, "what is it you want, here?"

"What do you mean, what do I want?"

"From us," said Lester. "What is it you want us to do for you? About Blackway?"

"Get him to stop what he's doing," said Lillian. "Get him to leave me alone."

"And how do you think we're going to do that?" Lester asked her. "Are we just going to talk to Blackway? Talk to his friends? Reason with them, with him? Argue Blackway into leaving you alone? Can we do that?"

"I don't know," said Lillian. "No. No, you can't."

Lester grinned at her and slapped his thigh. "Yes, we can," he said. "We can reason with Blackway." He turned to Nate and nodded. Nate started the engine, put the truck in gear, and got them headed around in the road.

"We can so argue with Blackway," Lester said. He reached down behind the seat and patted the parcel he'd laid on the floor back there.

"This here's the argument."

6

SHE LIKES IT HERE

"Kevin Bay," said Whizzer. "She was Kevin's girl. She and Kevin lived in a trailer there behind his folks. Past Dead River."

"She worked," said D.B. "Where did she work? At the inn, didn't she?"

"Waiting tables," said Coop.

"Holds herself pretty high for a waitress, don't she?" said D.B.

"It seems as though she worked at the school, too, for a while," said Whizzer.

"She was a teacher?" Conrad asked.

"No," said Coop. "Some kind of teacher's helper."

"Her and her *You people. What's the matter with you people?*" said D.B. "She's coming in pretty high for a girl wipes the little kids' asses at school."

"She's a bright girl," said Whizzer. "She worked at the nursery, too. Worked for Edie, there. Edie thought the world of her. No, she's a bright girl. Hard worker. Good thing, too."

"Good thing, with Kevin," said Coop.

"What I meant, wasn't it?" said Whizzer.

"Her boyfriend?" asked Conrad.

"Kevin was no prize, put it that way," D.B. said.

"I don't know about that," said Whizzer. "In school he was. Nobody ever said Kevin wasn't smart. Quick. Teachers wanted him to apply to college."

"Can you go to college in jail?" asked Coop.

"That's the thing," said D.B. "Kevin was smart, all right. He was too smart. He was the kind of smart that thinks everybody else is dumb."

"Kevin was a god damned mess, is what he was," said Coop. "Had a juvenile record about a hundred pages long. Turned eighteen, never looked back. Graduated, like."

"Funny how often you see that," said Conrad.

"See what?" Coop asked him.

"Blackway stopped him one night," said D.B.

"Stopped him?" asked Conrad.

"Blackway was one of Wingate's deputies," said Whizzer. "He stopped Kevin on Route Ten for operation of a vehicle with defective equipment."

"Headlight was out," said D.B.

"Stopped both of them," said Coop. "She was driving."

"That's right, too," said Whizzer. "She was. I forgot."

"Kevin had a bunch of dope in the car," said Coop. "Bunch of pot."

"Had it hidden away under the backseat," said D.B. "Where nobody would ever think to look for it."

"Clever kid," said Coop.

"I told you he was sharp," said Whizzer.

"Master criminal," said D.B.

"The girl didn't know Kevin had anything in the car," said Whizzer.

"She said she didn't know," said D.B.

"She didn't," said Whizzer.

"Blackway did, though," said Coop.

"Sure, he did," said Whizzer. "Blackway knew looking for

dope under Kevin Bay's backseat was like looking for ants at a picnic."

"Like looking for hot dogs at Fenway," said Coop.

"He also knew," Whizzer went on, "with Kevin's record and him being eighteen and not a juvenile anymore, he was in real trouble this time. He was going away."

"So he decided to work on him a little," said D.B. "Put a little weight on him. What do you call it?"

"You call it a shakedown," said Conrad.

"Decided to shake him down a little," said D.B.

"That's a thing Blackway has going for him," Whizzer said.

"Had going," said Coop.

"Had," said Whizzer. "Kind of a sideline he had. Deputy don't get paid much, you know."

"You got to hustle," said Coop

"You got to be an entrepreneur," said D.B.

"Blackway took the dope," said Whizzer.

"Confiscated it," said Coop.

"Impounded it," said D.B.

"Told Kevin he'd let him go this time," said Whizzer. "Told him it'd be a good idea for him to get clear out of town, because Blackway was going to be all over him from now on."

"Kevin did the smart thing," said D.B.

"First time in his life," said Coop.

"He took off. Where is Kevin? South, somewhere, ain't he?" asked Coop.

"Orlando," said Whizzer. "His dad's brother's down there. Kevin's working for him."

"Doing what?" asked Conrad.

"I couldn't tell you," Whizzer said.

"Keeping out of jail, it looks like," said D.B.

"Or not," said Coop.

"Or not," said D.B.

"What happened with the dope?" Conrad asked.

"Anybody's guess," said Coop.

"I wouldn't be surprised if it found its way to some of Blackway's friends," said D.B.

"Friends from out of state," said Coop.

"Associates," said D.B.

"Business connections Blackway's got here and there," said Coop.

"He left his girl behind, though, I guess?" Conrad said. "Kevin did."

"Well, that was the thing," said Whizzer. "Kevin takes off, but his girlfriend don't. She stays. Not only that, she files a complaint."

"Against Blackway," said Coop.

"Pistol, she is," said D.B.

"She goes to the troopers," said Coop.

"State police," said D.B.

"Tells them Deputy Blackway's got this thing going on the side where he smokes the evidence," said Coop.

"Sells the evidence," said D.B.

"Girl tells them she's a witness to Blackway doing that," said Coop.

"State police don't seem to get too excited by the news," said D.B.

"They remain calm," said Coop.

"Fact is, they knew all about it," said Whizzer.

"No, they didn't," said D.B. "They just didn't want to touch it.

Because of Wingate. Wingate's the sheriff. Blackway's his deputy. Wingate's responsible. They didn't want to make trouble for Wingate."

Whizzer laughed gently and shook his head at D.B.

"You don't think so?" asked D.B.

"Keep dreaming, son," said Whizzer.

"Point is," said Coop, "the troopers tell her it's a sheriff's department matter. Blackway ain't a state cop. He's a sheriff's deputy. Wingate's the sheriff."

"Wingate's Blackway's boss," said Whizzer.

"Plus, Wingate's about the only person in this part of the state who ain't scared shitless of Blackway," said Coop.

"Whizzer ain't scared of him," said D.B. "Are you, Whiz?"

"'Course not," said Whizzer. "I like Blackway."

"The girl turned him in," said Conrad. "She wasn't scared of him."

"She is now," said Coop.

"Nate the Great didn't seem to be scared of Blackway," Conrad said.

"He don't know no better," said Coop.

"Lester?" asked Conrad.

"Sure, Les is scared of Blackway," said Whizzer. "But Les is a clever old boy. He'll be ready."

"Les knows what he's doing," said Coop.

"Les knows a trick or two," said D.B.

"Point is," said Coop, "state police go to Wingate, explain to Wingate about Blackway's sideline, there, with the dope."

"Wingate fires Blackway," said Whizzer. "Turns Blackway into a civilian."

"No more car," said Coop.

"No more uniform," said D.B.

"No more gun," said Coop.

"No more evidence to impound for personal use or later sale to your friends from out of state," said Whizzer.

"All on account of that girl," said D.B.

"She pissed in his well," said Coop.

"Blackway's hot, now," said Whizzer.

"Kevin's long gone," said Coop.

"Followed the sun," said D.B.

"Girl's still here," said Whizzer.

"Why?" Conrad asked. "Why didn't she go with Kevin?"

"Didn't want to, it looks like," said Coop.

"Didn't get asked, maybe," said D.B.

"You heard her," said Whizzer. "She won't be run off. Not even by Blackway."

"Balls on her," said Coop.

"'Course, she don't know Blackway," said D.B.

"She does now," said Coop.

"Point is," said Whizzer, "Blackway ain't going to just let this one go. He wants to teach her a lesson."

"He watches her," said D.B.

"Follows her around," said Coop.

"Stalks her," said D.B.

"Like she said," said Coop.

"She ought to have left town when Kevin did, it looks like," said D.B.

"She ain't as smart as she thinks she is," said Coop.

"She's dumb, is what she is," said D.B.

"Edie didn't think she was dumb," said Whizzer. "When she

worked there. Edie thought real well of her. She got the place organized. Customers liked her. Edie thought she was a real bright girl."

"How bright could she be," D.B. asked, "getting together with Kevin?"

"But you see that over and over, here, don't you?" said Conrad. "I was saying before."

"See what?" Coop asked him.

"Where?" D.B. asked him.

"Here," said Conrad. "Around here. Women, young women, who are more or less bright, cleaned up, straight shooters, capable, strong. Want to work. Anyplace else, they'd end up with good solid young guys, guys just like them. But around here they go for guys who are the opposite, who are going nowhere except jail, who are nothing but trouble. They end up with guys who are trouble on skates. You see that a lot. Why?"

"Something in the water," said Coop.

"Winters are too long," said D.B.

"The young guys have this special aftershave they wear," said Coop.

"They don't want to be alone, the girls," said Whizzer.

"If that's what it was," said Coop, "it worked for What's-her-name."

"It worked too well," said D.B.

"Lillian," said Whizzer.

"Well," said D.B., "whatever it is she wanted, I don't see why she thought she'd find it here. Thinks she's so smart. *You people*. Cat named Annabelle. What kind of name's that for a cat? What's she doing around here in the first place?"

"She likes it here," said Whizzer.

"Just like Con," said Coop.

"But not so much," said Whizzer.

"No," said Coop. "Nobody likes it around here as much as Con. Ain't that right?"

"Nobody," said Conrad.

"Well," said Whizzer. "I don't know whether she's dumb or whether she's smart or whether she likes it here or she don't, but either way, here she is. And I'll tell you something else: It looks to me as though Blackway might have picked on the wrong girl this time."

7

THE DIAMOND JOB

Fitzgerald's job was on Diamond Mountain. His crew had been up there for three months. They had cleared out half an acre for the landing and built a lane into it for the trucks. Every day another truck, another two or three trucks, came out of the woods loaded as high as a house with fresh-cut logs. You would think there couldn't be a tree left standing on the mountain — not a tree in the town, in the state. And yet the woods were everywhere, untouched, unchanged, as though the abstracted logs, and the workings that produced them, were a magician's illusion.

Lillian, Lester, and Nate found the truck access to the landing, and Nate started to turn off the road.

"Back it in," said Lester.

Nate put the truck in reverse and backed into the log lane until they could see the landing.

"That's good," said Lester. Nate stopped the truck, stopped the engine. The three of them sat, with Lester turned around on the seat so he could see out the rear window.

"Is he there?" Lillian asked Lester.

"Don't see him," said Lester.

"Are you going in?" she asked.

"In a minute," said Lester.

He was watching the landing. There was a man there. He had seen them. He pointed to their truck. A second man joined him, then a third.

"How many of them are there?" Lillian asked.

"More than that," said Lester. To Nate he said, "Do you want to go ahead?"

"Yo," said Nate. He opened his door and left the truck. He began walking in toward the landing.

The landing was like a muddy amphitheater with the woods standing close all around. Its scarred, ruined earth was cut with deep ruts and tracks. Fitzgerald ran a neat job, though. There was a big pile of new gravel to one side of the landing for use in filling the ruts and keeping up the lane for the trucks. Around the woods edge, tops, waste logs, butt ends, and other slash had been bulldozed into piles the height of a tall man. Some of the oak butts were as big as bathtubs. There was nothing to do with them but get them out of the way. A hundred years from now they would still be lying right there.

Lester and Lillian looked out the rear window of the truck as Nate walked toward the landing. Four men now waited for him.

"None of them is Blackway," said Lillian.

"No," said Lester.

"What happens now?"

"Like Fitz said, maybe they know where Blackway is," said Lester.

"He just asks them?"

"It looks that way."

Nate had about reached the landing. Just within the woods he came upon a dog lying beside the lane in the shadows. It was a big one, one of those heavy, broad-shouldered breeds with a head the size of a small barrel and a great, dripping maw like a sea cave. It was on a chain fixed to a tree. The dog didn't get to its feet as Nate approached, but it watched him every second, and it let a low growl rise in its throat as Nate passed before it. Nate stared at the dog, but he didn't try to avoid it, and he didn't pause. He left it behind him and walked out into the landing.

The four loggers had strung themselves in a loose line in the middle of the landing to meet Nate. Two of them had axes on their shoulders, and a third carried one of the heavy poles, shod with an iron point and a hanging iron jaw or hook, that you use to move logs.

"Do you know them?" Lillian asked Lester.

"No," said Lester.

"Does he? Does Nate?"

Lester didn't take his eyes off the group at the landing.

"No," he said.

"What's going to happen?" Lillian asked him.

"Nothing."

"There's going to be a fight, isn't there?"

Lester glanced at her.

"Do you want a fight?" he asked her.

"No," said Lillian. "Not now. Four of them's too many."

"Kid reckons too many's about right," said Lester.

Nate walked into the landing. There were five loggers now. Blackway wasn't one of them. They made a half circle before Nate. The loggers were short, heavy men in dirty coveralls full of grease, sweat, and sawdust. They smelled of pine pitch and gasoline. Every one of them was chewing tobacco. Their jaw muscles worked slowly, in unison. None of them spoke. One of them, who stood in the middle of the group, with two others to each side of him, spat tobacco juice into the mud at his feet.

"Help you?" he asked Nate.

"Looking for Blackway," Nate said.

"Who's looking for him?"

"I am."

"Why?"

"We need to see him."

"We?"

"People with me," Nate said. "We need to talk to Blackway."

"I don't give a shit what you need," said the logger.

Nate looked from one of the five to the other, up and down their line. He grinned at them.

"Yo," said Nate.

He moved a little to his left, toward the nearer of the five loggers, who was also the smallest. He could roll them up from that side, if he had to — or he could try. But the five now moved themselves, coming together in a tighter group in front of Nate.

"That's right," said Lester, watching them from the truck. "Close it up, bunch it up. That's good." He opened his door and got out of the truck. He took his long parcel from behind the seat, but he didn't unwrap it. "Start it up," he said to Lillian. Lillian slid over behind the wheel and started the engine.

She watched Lester walk down the lane toward the landing. He limped, she saw, hitching his right leg stiffly. How old was he, really? Was he seventy? Was he eighty? Men like Lester, they do hard work outdoors all their lives, and the years, the weather break them down as though they were an old barn or an old truck: By the time they're middle-aged they're cripples. Lillian knew those men. Her own father might have used a rig like the one Whizzer had back at the mill. Maybe he had one by now. Lillian didn't know. She wasn't in touch with her family. She wasn't like them. They weren't like her. She had left them behind her when she had gone with Kevin.

Lillian watched Lester approach the landing. She saw him look to his right as he passed the dog lying beside the lane, but the dog itself she couldn't see from where she was. Lester left the woods and limped across the landing toward the spot where Nate faced the five loggers. Lillian watched him.

She had gone with Kevin because he was like her. He was like her, except that he was funny. She wasn't funny. She couldn't afford to be. Kevin was full of mockery. "East Schmuckville," he called their town. "You can't miss it," Kevin said. "It's exactly four miles south of West Schmuckville." He made her laugh.

Blackway put an end to that. Blackway stood in the night beside their car with the cruiser's lights popping and flashing and listened to Kevin blabbing away, trying to talk his way out of this one. Talk, talk, talk. Kevin thought he was so smart. "Is there a problem, Officer?" In two seconds Kevin was out of the car and slammed down on his face across the hood. Blackway was talking softly to him. Lillian had opened her door to get out of the car.

"Stay where you are, sweetheart," Blackway told her. She closed the door again.

Afterward Kevin shut right up. He wouldn't talk to her, he wouldn't talk at all. Lillian asked him what Blackway had said to him the night of the stop. Kevin wouldn't tell her. He was no longer funny. He no longer made her laugh. He wouldn't leave the house. Then one day she got home from work and he was gone. No note, no word. Kevin just put his little tail down and ran. Well, fuck him, then. Fuck Kevin. He wanted to run? Let him run.

The five men in front of Nate heard the truck start. They looked past Nate. They saw Lester coming toward them up the log lane. He had the long parcel tucked under his right arm with one end snug against his side and the other pointing to the ground in front of his feet.

"Who's that?" the middle logger asked Nate.

"He's looking for Blackway, too," Nate said.

Lester came up beside Nate and stood to his right about four feet away from him and no more than seven or eight feet from the loggers.

"You ask them?" he said to Nate.

"Yo," Nate said.

"What's that you got in there?" the middle logger asked Lester.

"We been to Fitz's," Lester said. "Fitz told us we might find him up here. Might find Blackway. That's what Fitz said, ain't it?" he asked Nate.

"Yo," Nate said.

"Blackway ain't here," said the logger. "What's that?" he asked Lester again.

"This, here?" Lester said. "Curtain rods."

"Bullshit, curtain rods," said the logger.

Lester raised the end of his parcel so it pointed about at the knees of the group of five loggers.

"Blackway hasn't been here today, at all, I guess?" he said.

"He was here," said the small logger. "Might be he's gone up to the High Line."

"Why don't you shut up?" said the middle logger.

"Why don't you?" said the small one. "You see what he's got. He never told us nothing about not telling nobody where he was. Let him worry about them."

"You fellows go on back to work," said Lester. "We've taken up too much of your time. Fitz will dock your pay."

The middle logger spat onto the ground between them. "Fitz won't dock nobody," he said.

"Probably not," said Lester. "We're much obliged to you. We'll try the High Line."

The five held their ground, but they looked at one another, then at the logger in the middle of their line. Lester lifted the parcel again so its end pointed at the middle logger's belt buckle.

"Go on, now," said Lester.

The small logger and three of the others turned and started toward the woods. The middle logger turned, too, then turned back to them. He spat into the mud again.

"He ain't hiding from you," he said.

"Go on," said Lester.

"You find him, you're going to wish you hadn't," said the other.

Lester didn't reply. The logger turned away. Nate and Lester waited until the five were most of the way across the landing. Then they returned to the truck and Lillian. The great dog lay beside the lane with its head on its paws and watched them go.

"What happened?" said Lillian. She moved from behind the wheel, and Nate took the driver's place.

"Get going," said Lester. They drove out of the log landing and turned onto the road.

"Blackway went to the High Line," Lester said.

"What's the High Line?" Lillian asked.

"Well, it's like a motel, I guess you'd say," Lester said.

Nate snickered.

"We're going there?" Lillian said.

"It looks that way," said Lester. "Unless you'd rather bag this whole business. In that case, we can drop you back at Whizzer's."

"No," said Lillian. "What happened back there?"

"Not much."

"I thought there was going to be a fight."

"No fight," said Lester. "Those fellows mostly look harder than they fight."

"That's a gun you've got in there, isn't it?"

"They thought so," Lester said.

"You tricked them, then," said Lillian. "That's why there was no fight. Either that's a gun and you scared them off or it isn't and you made them think it was. Either way it was nothing but a trick. You were afraid to fight all of them, so you tricked them so you wouldn't have to."

"Who was afraid?" Nate asked her.

"What have you got against tricks?" Lester asked her.

"I wasn't afraid," Nate said.

"What's she got against tricks?" Lester asked Nate.

Lillian was silent.

"Don't know," said Nate.

"She don't like tricks," Lester said.

"She likes fights," Nate said.

"Thing is, it ain't her has to do the fighting," said Lester.

"No," said Nate. "No, it ain't her."

"Do you think you could give it a rest?" Lillian asked them. "No, I didn't want a fight. Five against one isn't a fight."

"It ain't?" asked Nate.

"Five against two, wasn't it?" asked Lester.

"Okay," said Lillian. "Five against two. Anyway, I'm glad there was no fight. Okay?"

"Okay with me," said Lester.

"No fight — this time," said Lillian.

"Mind you," said Lester. "I like a good fight, myself. But it's a young fellow's game, ain't it? Fighting? Like my wife and me, when we were young, God, we fought all the time. Just married: We'd fight about anything. I mean fight, too: shouting, screaming, throwing things — all day and all night. Then when we got old, it seemed like we simmered down. Don't fight anywhere near as much anymore."

"You tricked them," said Lillian. "You won't trick Blackway."

"'Course," Lester went on, "that might be partly because she moved out on me."

"Did you see that dog?" Nate asked Lester.

"What dog?" asked Lillian.

"I saw him," said Lester.

"I didn't see any dog," said Lillian.

"He was in the woods," Lester said. "Must be one of them fellow's dogs. Just sat there, didn't make a sound. I hate a dog that never barks."

"Awhile ago you said you hated dogs that do bark," said Lillian.

"He don't like dogs, it looks like," said Nate.

"Big bastard, too, wasn't he?" said Lester. "Dog that size, you don't know whether to put a saddle on him or milk him."

"You want to milk that one," said Nate, "you're on your own."

8

STILL RUNNING

"Well," said D.B., "if she likes it here so much, she's got a funny way of showing it. *You people.* Thinks she's some trick. Cat named Annabelle. Hair down to her ass."

"What's it to you what she calls her cat?" Coop asked him.

"Can't get around that hair, can you?" said Whizzer.

"Look," said Coop, "at least she had most of her clothes on. Girls you see today go around half naked."

"They do?" Whizzer asked.

"Sure," said Coop. "And, look: At least she don't have herself stuck all full of nuts and bolts like so many of them you see."

"Nuts and bolts?" Whizzer asked.

"Piercing," said D.B. "I don't understand that, do you? And that ain't all. There's the jewelry. Other day I was at the clinic, getting blood drawn. Little girl works there, that Rowena, takes your blood? She had this thing on, this shirt, showed her belly, and in there she had a diamond, right in her belly button. I mean, she wore it to work."

"A diamond?" Whizzer asked.

"It's a fake, Whiz," said Coop. "It had to be. Nobody wears a real diamond in her belly like that. She'd be afraid she'd lose it."

"Well, maybe the diamond was a fake," said D.B., "but her belly button was real, and the diamond was right in there."

"How does she get it to stay put?" Whizzer asked. "Glue?"

"That's no glue," said Coop. "It's in there like an earring. It's another piercing. You stick a needle in there, make a hole, like in your ear. Then you hang your diamond on that, it's on a little ring."

"I didn't see no ring on it," said D.B.

"You didn't get close enough," said Coop.

"Close enough to see about everything else she had," said D.B. "That's what I'm saying. What happened to the way these little girls dress themselves, you know? What about these kids you see today in school? Piercing? Bellies? Diamonds? I'm talking about girls twelve, thirteen years old. Not even high school. They dress the same way: You've got the little thing on top with the straps, you've got the bare belly, the tight jeans. That kind of outfit, you used to have to pay money to see. You used to have to pay money and sit in the dark. Now you go into any middle school. What about that?"

"What about it?" asked Conrad.

Whizzer chuckled. "All them bellies," he said. "Them diamonds, rings. All that skin. This young fellow don't approve, it looks like. He don't, really."

"What about you?" Conrad asked Whizzer. "Do you approve?'

"I do," said Whizzer. "I am for it."

"So am I, mostly," said D.B. "I like to look, much as the next fellow. Have to say, though, it's different when it's your kid. Like just this past year? First day of school? Our Amy? Shows up wearing a skirt that you could pretty near see what she'd had for breakfast. Junior high, this is. She's headed for the bus. 'Wait just a god damned minute, here,' I said."

"That's what I'm saying," said Coop.

"I told her there's no way in hell she's leaving the house in that outfit," said D.B.

"Uh-oh," said Whizzer.

"That's just what I'm saying," said Coop.

"Uh-oh, is right," said D.B. "I mean, she starts crying and wailing and carrying on. All the other kids dress like that. Do I want her to not have friends? And her mom? Her mom takes her part. What's the big deal? Everybody does it. Do I want our kid to be different? God damned right, I do. Neither one of them spoke to me or even looked at me for a month."

"But she changed her clothes," said Coop.

"She did," said D.B.

"That's what I'm saying," said Coop. "Where are these kids' parents? It ain't the kids' fault. They don't know no better. Nobody expects them to. But where are their parents?"

"If my sister?" said D.B. "If my sister had tried to go to school in an outfit like that when we were kids, my dad would have whipped her, and my mom would have held her down while he did it."

"Do that today and see what happens," said Conrad.

"You'll have Wingate knocking on your door," said Coop.

"Wingate?" said D.B.

"That's what I'm saying," said Coop. "He's right. Con's right. You would have Wingate knocking on your door, protecting your fifteen-year-old kid's God-given right to go around like a hooker. The law is on her side."

"Wingate wouldn't knock on your door," said Whizzer. "Not really. He'd find some way to work things out. Sit down, talk things over. He'd try, anyway."

"Wingate likes to talk," said Coop. "I'll give you that. He just don't like to do. Like with Blackway, there."

"I thought Wingate sacked Blackway," said Conrad.

"He did," said Whizzer. "Fired his ass. What are you talking about?" he asked Coop.

"What's-her-name," said Coop. "Lillian. I'm talking about her. She went to Wingate. Before she came here. She just told you. Wingate told her there's nothing he can do. He gave her the law."

"That's his job," said Whizzer.

"She went to him for help, and he gave her the law," said Coop. "That don't do her a lot of good with Blackway, does it? Blackway don't care about the law. He just does what he wants. He just goes for it."

"Wingate's the sheriff," said Whizzer. "What do you want him to do, saddle up and go out after Blackway on his own because of what some girl says? You know he can't do that."

"Why not?" Coop said. "Why can't he — if he knows what she says is true? And he does. Everybody knows it. Everybody knows Blackway. How he does. What he is."

"Wingate can't do that," said Whizzer.

"Why can't he?" Coop demanded. "Face it, Whiz: Wingate's no ball of fire. He's all right for what he has to do, mostly. Serving papers and writing up speeding tickets? Sure. He's a plugger. But face it: He ain't the sharpest guy that ever came along."

"Not like Blackway, you mean?" asked Conrad.

"Not like Blackway," said Coop. "Do I mean Blackway's sharp? Smart? Well, I don't know. He's smarter than Wingate, anyway. Ain't he? Wingate just goes along, picking them up and putting them down. Blackway? Look, Blackway sees something he wants, he takes it. If you don't like that and you think you can take it back, you're welcome to try. That's all. With Blackway, law don't really come into it, much."

"Blackway's kind of beyond the law, I guess," said Conrad.

"There you go," said Coop. "Wingate?" he went on, "Wingate's strictly by-the-book. All right, he has to be. But I'll say it again: Wingate ain't the brightest guy in the world. He goes by the book because he don't have what it takes to do different. The — what would you call it? To do different. Ain't that brains?"

"That's imagination," said Conrad.

"There you go," said Coop. "He ain't got the imagination."

"Wingate's got a job to do," said Whizzer. "He's an officer of the law. He don't get paid to imagine."

"That's what I'm saying," said Coop.

"That ain't being stupid, though," said Whizzer.

"Ain't it?" Coop demanded. "Ain't it? Look, you take that thing where Wingate fired Blackway. Okay, Blackway busts some kid and takes his dope and sells it. So what? Who's hurt?"

"It's against the law," said Whizzer.

"So what if it is?" said Coop. "So what? What difference does it make? Somebody else smokes that particular bunch of dope, that's all. You think the law, you think Wingate, can make any difference to that? You know he can't. People want dope, or anything else, they'll find a way to get it."

"Blackway's glad to help them," said D.B.

"He's a benefactor," said Conrad.

"I didn't say that," said Coop.

"Didn't you?" said D.B. "I thought you did."

"We've got two different arguments going here, don't we?" asked Conrad.

"At least," said Whizzer.

"I make it three," said D.B.

"I ain't arguing nothing," said Coop. "I only said Wingate's a plugger — nothing against him — and Blackway's a stand-up guy in his own way."

"You better hope he ain't standing on you, then," said Whizzer.

Coop laughed. "Yeah, well, I won't fight with you on that one, I don't guess," he said.

"Best to leave Blackway alone," said D.B.

"Even if you're Wingate," said Coop.

"So, I guess she did right to come here for help, didn't she?" said Conrad. "Lillian. She came to the right place, I guess. Anyway, there wasn't anyplace else for her to go. It's too bad Scott Cavanaugh wasn't here. To help her."

Whizzer chuckled. "Scotty might not think so," he said.

"Scotty knows Blackway," said Coop.

"I guess he does," said D.B. "Do you remember that thing at the Fort that time?"

"I was there," said Coop.

"What thing?" Conrad asked them.

"God," said Whizzer. "Ten years ago? Twelve?"

"More," said Coop.

"What was it?" Conrad asked.

"Oh," Coop said, "Scotty and his brother and a couple of their friends got into it with Blackway one night at the Fort. I never knew why. There were four of them. Blackway was by himself. They figured the numbers were about right. They went after him."

"Big mistake," said D.B.

"Big one," Coop agreed. "Blackway put three of them in the hospital. Scotty had his jaw wired up for a couple of months. Couldn't eat stuff. One of his friends didn't come to for three days."

"What did he do to them?" Conrad asked.

"Kicked Scotty's brother in the balls," said Coop. "He was the only one didn't have to go to the hospital."

"No permanent damage," said D.B. "Had to hurt, though."

"Scotty swung at Blackway," Coop said. "Blackway took it on his shoulder and gave him one right back. That was it for Scotty. Broke his jaw. One of the other guys Blackway hit with something."

"Some kind of a bar he had," said Whizzer.

"It wasn't a bar," Coop said. "It was a chair. He hit him with a chair."

"He hit him with a thing like a tire iron," Whizzer said.

"He hit him with a chair," Coop said.

"Might have been a jack handle," said Whizzer. "Made of steel, couple of feet long."

"He hit him with a chair, Whiz," said Coop. "He picked up a chair and hit him with it. I was there."

"So was I," said Whizzer.

"You were?" said Coop. "Where were you?"

"Coming out of the gents'," said Whizzer. "I could walk then."

"Where were you?" Conrad asked Coop.

"Looking for the exit," said Coop. "Me and everybody else in the place. Whole thing took about half a minute."

"What happened to the fourth one?" Conrad asked. "Scotty had his jaw broken. His brother got kicked in the balls. His one friend was out for three days. What happened to the other?"

"Still running," said Whizzer.

"So, we're saying Nate and Lester can take on Blackway when those four couldn't?" Conrad asked.

"I ain't saying it," said Coop.

"I ain't saying it," said D.B.

"They got a shot," said Whizzer. "That was a long time ago. Blackway's not as young as he was. Nate the Great's got twenty years on him, more than that. Plus, he's bigger."

"He ain't a lot bigger," said D.B.

"Bigger enough," said Whizzer. "And strong? You remember that thing with Perry and his car."

"What thing?" Conrad asked.

"Perry's car rolled onto him," said D.B.

"He had a flat," said Coop. "On the river road. Had a flat, got out, got the thing jacked up. An Escort, it was."

"Chevette," said Whizzer.

"It was an Escort," said Coop. "White."

"It was white," said Whizzer. "But it was a Chevette."

"What happened?" Conrad asked.

"Slipped the jack," said D.B.

"Car slipped off the jack," said Coop, "knocked Perry over, rolled onto his arm, stopped."

"Pinned him," said D.B.

"There he was," said Coop.

"Couldn't move," said Whizzer. "Along came Nate the Great, on his way to work."

"Stopped," said D.B.

"Perry asked him to go for help," said Coop, "or get the jack and raise the car up off his arm."

"Nate the Great says, sure," said Whizzer. "But he don't go for help. He don't get the jack. He just gets around front of the car, takes hold of the bumper, and lifts the whole god damned car up so Perry can get his arm out from under."

"He's holding the car up there, and he tells Perry to take his time," says Coop.

" 'Take your time,' says Nate the Great," Whizzer said. "What I'm saying, he's a pretty rugged kid. He's holding the Chevette up in the air like it's nothing."

"The Escort," said Coop.

"Nate the Great can give Blackway a run," said Whizzer.

Coop shook his head. "I ain't saying the kid don't have the grunts," he said. "But he ain't clever. He'll think he's in some kind of a prizefight. He won't know to kick or to pick up a chair."

"A bar," said Whizzer.

"Okay, Whiz," said Coop. "It was a bar. It was a Chevette. Are you happy now? What I mean, that kid don't know the tricks."

"No," said Whizzer, "but Les does."

"What tricks?" Conrad asked.

"Whatever ones it takes," said D.B.

"You wait," said Whizzer. "Les knows all the tricks, and then he knows a couple more. And I'll tell you something else: Les'll go through. He'll go all the way through. Hell, come to that, Les is as crazy as Blackway."

9

FRIENDS OF BLACKWAY

The High Line Cabins are gone today. They stood about at the top of Route 10, where you turn off to take the road into the mountain country to the north. The highway went down a hill and into a curve there, and the crossing road came in just at the bend: a bad spot. Lately the state highway department has gone to work on that stretch. They have taken out the curve, they have taken out the hill — and they have taken out the High Line Cabins. Even the place where they were, you could say, has ceased to exist.

Few mourn. The High Line was not a good place. A sad, dirty, half-empty place, the habitat of sad, dirty, half-empty people, people who didn't want to be seen: runaways, suicides, drinkers, addicts, sellers of goods that are on no account to be sold. In particular the High Line catered to adulterers. Restless citizens of Bennington, Rutland, Brattleboro went there with women who weren't their wives, with men who weren't their friends. Weekends, you didn't even have to bring a woman with you to the High Line; the women would be set up there on their own. All you had to do was sit in your car and wait your turn. Then, the High Line amounted to an old-fashioned whorehouse, without the piano and without the warmhearted, middle-aged female boss. Some of the local people called it Tailtown.

Lillian and the two men turned into the parking lot at the High Line. Nate stopped the truck in front, and they sat and watched the building for a minute.

"This is the place?" Lillian asked.

"This is it," said Lester.

"What a dump," Lillian said. "People pay to stay here?"

"Not for very long," Lester said. "Hah. What I mean, not for very long — at a stretch. Ain't that right?" he asked Nate.

"Yo," said Nate.

The High Line wasn't a big place. It sat on an acre or less, a gravel lot on the road front and a patch of weeds and brush behind, festive with paper wrappings, empty cartons, empty cans and bottles, used-up rubber products, other trash. The building held twenty units in a two-decker range with stairs on each end to get you up to a balcony that led to the second-story rooms. The place was painted white with a green roof, green doors to the rooms. Maybe that paint job was intended to charm. Maybe it was intended to summon the prim, clean order of the Vermont village. It didn't. For the High Line and places like it, you can paint them any color you want, and what they mostly look like is a state prison for the half bad.

"Well," Lester said.

Nate opened the driver's door and got out of the truck.

"You probably want to wait out here," Lester said to Lillian.

"I'm not sitting out here alone," said Lillian.

"Suit yourself," said Lester. He left the truck and turned toward the building.

"Aren't you going to take your gun?" Lillian asked him.

"Gun?" Lester asked.

"That's right," said Lillian. "Your package? Aren't you going to bring it?"

Lester paused. He seemed to consider. Then he shook his head.

"I guess not this time," he said.

The three of them had started toward the building when a door marked OFFICE in the near end of the first floor opened, and a tall man stood in front of it looking at them. He was a big one, all right: six and a half feet high and in no way skinny, with a long tangled beard that hung from his chin to his chest. The beard was black at the sides and gray down the middle and made the man look like he was in the act of eating a skunk headfirst.

The bearded man approached them.

"Where do you think you're going?" he said.

Nate took a step toward him and turned a little, so his left shoulder was toward the man. But then Lester said, "Hello, Stu."

The man looked past Nate to Lester. "Oh, yeah," he said.

"How have you been, Stu?" Lester asked.

"What do you want?" asked the man.

"Blackway," said Lester. "We're looking for Blackway."

"What for?"

"He'll want to see us," Lester said. He looked at Nate. "Ain't that right?" he asked Nate.

"That's right," said Nate.

"That's right," said Lester. "Blackway's a lucky man today. We've got some good news for Blackway. He'll want to see us."

"He ain't here," said Stu. "He was, but he left."

"That's too bad," Lester said. "Ain't that too bad?" he said to Nate.

"That's too bad," Nate said.

"Blackway will be hot about missing us," Lester said. "Won't he?"

"He will," said Nate.

"He won't be happy," said Lester.

"He won't," said Nate.

"His partner's here," said Stu. "You can see him."

Just then a woman in a room on the second floor began to laugh. She began, and she didn't stop: a high, clear, unhinged laugh as though she was being tickled. She laughed until she ran out of breath, then she started in again.

"*Hee-hee-heee-heee. Oh, hee-heee-heee.*"

"What did you say?" Lester asked.

"You can see his partner," said Stu. He turned and led them up a flight of concrete steps to the second-floor balcony and along it to a room halfway down. He knocked on the door. It opened immediately. A man stood in the doorway, filling it. In the adjoining room the woman's laughter went on and on. The man in the door stepped back out of the way. Nate, Lester, and Lillian followed Stu into the room.

In the room there were four men. One sat in a chair at a credenza against the wall to the left. The others stood: one beside the bed, one in the corner beyond the bed, and the fourth, who had let them in, near the door. On the bed were two large suitcases.

All the lights in the room were on. There was a big window in the wall opposite the door, but its heavy drapes were closed tight.

The man standing beside the bed was snapping shut the lid of one of the suitcases when the three of them entered behind Stu.

The man sitting at the credenza looked up at them. He blinked. "Uh, who are they?" he asked.

From the next room the crazy woman's noise was louder than it had been out on the balcony. It wasn't laughter now, but a broken wail, a howl as of the world's lonesomest coyote on the world's lonesomest prairie. "Say what?" asked Stu.

"Who are they?"

"Looking for Blackway," said Stu.

"*Yoo-ooo-woo-wooo-wooo.*"

"What?" said the man at the credenza. "Which one is that?" he asked Stu.

"That'd be Delphine," said Stu.

"Can't you shut her up?" he asked.

"You know Delphine."

"*Yoo-ooo-woo-wooo-wooo.*"

"I'll get her," said the man by the door. He left the room. Shortly the howling next door shot up into a little shriek and then fell quickly away to silence, as when you lift a whistling teakettle quickly off the fire.

The man sitting at the credenza took a cigarette from a package at his elbow and put it in his mouth. Stu stepped forward and lit it for him with a metal lighter. The man puffed his cigarette, and Stu closed the lighter with a loud snap and stepped back to his place. "They're looking for Blackway," he told the seated man.

The man at the credenza was middle-sized. He wore a brown leather jacket. He had a round, bewildered face, and he stared at them as though he weren't fully awake and responded to what was said to him only after a certain delay, as though he had to wait for a translation. He smoked his cigarette.

"They're looking for Blackway," Stu said again.

"Blackway isn't here," said the seated man.

"You know where we can find him?" Lester asked.

The man who had gone next door to quiet the crazy woman came back into the room and took his place by the door.

The sleepy man at the credenza gazed at Lester, but he didn't reply.

"You know where Blackway is?" Lester asked him again.

The man shook his head slowly from side to side. "You know them, at all?" he asked Stu.

"I know him," said Stu, looking at Lester. "Sure."

"Her?" the man at the credenza asked.

"No," said Stu. "Could get to know her, though."

The man in the corner grinned. Nate turned to look at Stu, but Lester put a hand on his shoulder.

"The thing is," said Lester, "we need to see Blackway."

The man at the credenza turned to him. "Blackway isn't here," he said again.

"You said."

The other let the ash on his cigarette drop onto the carpet.

"Uh, what do you want with Blackway?" he asked.

"Well, the thing is, he won," Lester said. "Didn't he?" he asked Nate.

"He did," said Nate.

The man blinked. After a moment he said, "Won?"

"He won the raffle," said Lester.

"Uh, raffle?"

"That's right," said Lester. "The fire department raffle. You know."

"I do?"

"Blackway won it," said Nate.

"He won part of it," said Lester. "Didn't he?" he asked Nate.

"That's right," Nate said. "He won the VCR."

"He didn't either win the VCR," said Lester. "He won the gas grill."

"That was Denny won the grill," said Nate. "Blackway won the VCR."

"You're thinking of last year," Lester said. "Denny won the grill last year."

The man at the credenza gazed from one to the other of them. "VCR?" he said.

"That was the year before," Nate said. "Denny won the cord of wood last year."

"Jesus fucking Christ!" said the man beside the bed. He hadn't spoken before, but now he said, "Jesus fucking Christ! You fucking woodchucks got all the time in the world up here, don't you? Are we going to do some business, here, today? This week? Is this some kind of a fucking party, here?"

"No," said the man at the credenza. "Okay, okay," he said to Lester. "Blackway was here. He was going by the Fort. You know the Fort? He had to see a guy at the Fort. He might be there. Or he might have gone ahead up to his place, up the mountain. His camp. You want him, I'd go to the Fort, then if he isn't there, I'd go to his place. You know where that is?"

"We know," Lester said.

The man at the credenza blinked. "I don't," he said. "I don't know where that is," he said. "Uh, you know where that is?" he asked the man standing at the door.

"All the time in the fucking world," the man by the bed said. "Hey, why don't we get a few more in here? You know? We could have a party. Why don't we send out for fucking pizza?" He slapped his hand down on one of the suitcases that lay on the bed. "Can we move this?" he demanded. "I've got a long drive."

The seated man looked at the big bearded man, Stu. "Get them out of here," he said.

"Blackway stops back here, tell him about the gas grill, okay?" said Lester.

"About the VCR," said Nate.

"Okay, okay," said the other.

The man at the door turned and opened it, and the three of them left the room, followed by Stu. They stood on the balcony outside.

"That was Blackway's partner, you said?" Lester asked Stu.

"That was nobody," Stu said.

"I mean the one who was talking," Lester said.

"Nobody was talking," said Stu. "Go on, now. Go on home. If I was you, I'd go right on home. Forget about Blackway. Give the — what? — the TV to somebody else. Blackway don't need a TV."

"Gas grill," said Lester. "We can't. Blackway won it. It's his. We've got to get it to him."

"You want Blackway, go to the Fort," said Stu. "If he ain't there, Murdock will be. He's buddies with Blackway. He'll know where he is. See Murdock."

"Murdock?" Lester asked. "Is he back?"

"Since spring," said Stu.

In the next room the crazy woman began to laugh again, opening with a low chuckle but soon rising to the full, howling hysteria of her earlier performance. Did she, maybe, think she was singing?

"There she goes again," said Stu. He slammed his fist against the woman's door, but her laughter continued.

"Get out of here," said Stu.

They left him on the balcony and went down the stairs and across the lot to the truck. Stu watched them from the balcony until they had driven out of the lot. Lillian turned in the seat to look behind.

"He's watching us," she said. "What a toad."

"You mean Stu?" Lester asked.

"All of them. You know him?"

"I did," Lester said. "Some time ago. We worked on the same woods crew one year. Part of the year — until he quit. Young Stu was never what you'd call a hard worker."

"What a bunch of toads," Lillian said. "I feel like I need a bath just being in the same room with them. And that woman next door? My God, what was going on in there?"

"Couldn't say," said Lester.

"Do you know this Murdock he was talking about?" Lillian asked Lester.

"Seen him," said Lester. "He's a prize steer, Murdock is. He was in prison, somewhere in the south. Too bad for us."

"That he was in prison?" asked Lillian.

"That they let him out."

"I ain't scared of him," said Nate.

"'Course you ain't," said Lester.

"I wasn't worried back in there, either," said Nate. "I wasn't worried about the big one, Stu. If he'd started something, I had him."

"He was twice as big as you," said Lillian.

"He was soft," Nate said.

"That other one, though," Lester said. "The one did the talking. He was different."

"He was zoned," said Lillian. "He was on Valium or something."

"What's Valium?" Lester asked.

"I bet they were all zoned," Lillian went on, "or we wouldn't have gotten out of there. You wouldn't have been able to blow all that raffle garbage by them. That was the stupidest thing I ever heard. It was like something Kevin would try."

"Who's Kevin?" Lester asked.

"It was just like Kevin," Lillian went on. "Nothing but talk. Nothing but words."

"Worked, didn't it?" Lester said.

"It worked because the big one is too dumb to move, and the rest of them were wasted," Lillian said. "We were in trouble in there. You tricked them — again. You did it again. If you'd had to fight them, it would have been different."

"Stu ain't so dumb," said Lester. "I wouldn't say Stu was dumb. Not smart, maybe, but not that dumb."

"What about the other two?" Lillian asked Nate. "I suppose you weren't worried about them, either?"

Nate didn't reply.

"Look," said Lillian. "That's two times you've been able to sneak around without a fight. Do you think you can do that much longer?"

"Hope not," Nate said.

Lester laughed. "Me, too," he said. "You just wait till I turn this kid loose. You'll see something then."

"You'll turn him loose?" asked Lillian. "And how about you? You wouldn't have been much help, would you? You didn't bring your gun with you."

"Gun?" asked Lester.

"You didn't bring it," said Lillian.

"No," said Lester.

"Why not?" Lillian asked.

"Gun's only good when it's the only gun," Lester said.

10

A MUSEUM OF WHAT?

D.B. shook his head. "Les ain't crazy," he said.

"He just spent a little too much time working too far out in the woods, it looks like," said Coop.

"Got hit by one too many falling trees," said D.B.

"Like me," said Whizzer.

"You said it," said Coop, "not me."

"But I ain't crazy," said Whizzer.

"You said it," said D.B., "not me."

"No," said Whizzer, "but yes: Les put in his time out there. He worked for Fitz's dad — hell, he might have worked for his granddad. Les worked in the woods when they had horses."

"He doesn't look that old," said Conrad. "How old is he?"

"Older than me," said Whizzer.

"Nobody's older than you," said Coop.

"I remember Les as a kid," Whizzer said. "When we were kids. He used to hang around Lucas's shop, help with the shoeing."

"Lucas's shop?" asked Conrad.

"Lucas's," said Coop. "Blacksmith shop. Used to be just this side of the bridge, on the right, there."

"Place that's an antiques shop now," said Whizzer. "The Forge."

"Oh, that place," said Conrad. "You know, that's another thing."

"What is?" asked D.B.

"Les helped around the shop," Whizzer went on. "Some people said he lived there, at Lucas's, upstairs or in the coal shed, there."

"What's another thing?" D.B. asked Conrad.

"Wait," said Conrad.

"Les didn't really have anyplace to go, he didn't have a home, it didn't look like," said Whizzer. "He just kind of turned up one day, only a kid. Slept at Lucas's, slept wherever he could. Slept here, probably."

"Kind of a Huck Finn," said Conrad.

"Kind of," said Whizzer.

"Who?" asked D.B.

"Who?" asked Coop.

"He had no family?" Conrad asked Whizzer.

"If he did," Whizzer said, "nobody knew who they were. He hung around, did one thing and another."

"He was a kid," said Conrad. "Didn't he go to school?"

"It don't seem like he did," said Whizzer. "Who was going to send him? But he knew something about horses, and by and by he went to work in the woods."

"What's another thing?" D.B. asked Conrad.

"Well," said Conrad, "how everything around here used to be something else. Like the antiques shop was a blacksmith's. Our house? Our house was a schoolhouse, Betsy says."

"That's right," said Whizzer. "That's right, it was."

"So what?" asked D.B.

"Well," said Conrad. "It strikes me, that's all. Everything's switched around. The blacksmith's an antiques shop, the school's somebody's house . . ."

"That place on the way to the Fort," said Coop. "That basket store. That was — what?"

"Dr. Osgood's office, when I was a kid," said Whizzer.

"The Fort itself, come to that," said Coop. "The Fort used to be a garage, go back far enough."

"It did," said Whizzer.

"But so what?" asked D.B.

"Well," said Conrad, "it's this change you've got going here. Nothing's what it started out as. Everything's changed around. You know? You've got this — I don't know. This flux."

"You better watch your mouth, there, young fellow," said Coop. "You're starting to sound like What's-her-name."

"Except for here," said Whizzer.

"That's right," said D.B. "This place has been here — how long?"

"Long time," said Whizzer.

"A long time, and always the same," said D.B.

"But not forever, maybe," said Conrad.

"How do you mean?" D.B. asked. "Why not?"

"Con's right," said Coop. "Who knows what's going to happen to this place? Come to that, you could do a lot here, you wanted to."

"I know it," said Whizzer. "Place is loaded with potential. What it is, though, is there's a lack of capital."

"Think about it, though," said D.B. "You could turn it into some kind of a museum."

"A museum of what?" Coop asked him.

"I ain't got that far," said D.B.

"You got to move into the present day, here," Coop told D.B. "You want the whole world to be a museum. I'm thinking apartments, here, you know, condos. Maybe with an outfit to it like a gym. What is it you call that?"

"A fitness center?" Conrad asked.

"There you go," said Coop. "Put in a fitness center."

"I'm thinking we move some girls in here," said Whizzer. "Set them right up: beds, hot water. Put in a Coke machine. Make a little run at Stu and them, up there on the highway."

"We'll all go to jail," said Conrad, "but it's your place."

"Or, here's what you do," Coop said. "How about this? Sell the whole works off to that place down in Mass, that old-time town."

"Sturbridge Village," said Conrad.

"There you go," said Coop. "Sell her to Sturbridge. Lock, stock, and barrel. They come up, put the whole works on a flatbed, the whole mill, and move it right down there. Set it up again, charge admission."

"I like it," said Conrad.

"Come to that," said D.B. "They could move us along with the rest."

"Package deal," said Coop.

"So you're saying we'd just sit around, down at What's-its-name?" asked Whizzer. "Sturbridge? Let the tourists look at us? Just be there?"

"Why not?" said Coop. "That's all we do here."

"What are we talking about for money, do you reckon?" Whizzer asked.

"Millions, Whiz," said Coop.

"Millions," said Conrad. "You've got to look at what this is, here. This is no Disneyland business, you know. This is no stage set. This is the real thing."

"You think?" Whizzer asked him.

11

FORT BOB

A mile and a half past the village as you go toward Dead River Settlement, you see on your left a big, high old house, like a haunted house, once grand but now a slum, with a broken window patched over by cardboard, a mangy slate roof, and sagging porches all around. A place with a story to it, you think, and maybe you're right. Maybe it is. No matter. Pass it by.

Not that place, and not the next one, Bea's Baskets & Birdhouses, but the place beyond them on the same side of the road is a low gray building made of cement blocks, a kind of bunker. It was put up years ago to house an auto repair business, but that enterprise failed, and for many years since the building has been a bar called, by the sign on the road, the Hill Country Inn — by everyone else Fort Bob.

The Fort was not the kind of bar where a good Mormon or a good Muslim could get a glass of water. It was not the kind of bar where you stopped for a drink on your way home from work. It was the kind of bar where you stopped for many drinks on your way to work, until soon enough they fired you and you could spend the whole day at the Fort. In converting the building from a garage to a bar, Bob, the owner, hadn't given a lot of thought to charm. He had walled over the three bay doors using glass blocks at a height of six feet. These were the only thing in the building answering to windows, and each of them held an electric beer sign. You couldn't see into the Fort, and you couldn't see out — but in either case why would you want to?

Inside the Fort were a long bar, five booths, and eight tables. There was no pool table, no pinball. There was a record machine in the corner, but it was unplugged. You didn't go to the Fort to play games, you didn't go there to listen to music. At the Fort you put away childish things. The Fort was a plain, businesslike place, a factory for the manufacture and upkeep of drunks. It did not have a good name, but at the time it was the only establishment of its kind in the district.

Nate turned off the road and drove along the front of the Fort. He parked the truck at a corner of the building, near the door. Seven cars and three motorcycles were parked in front.

"Blackway drives a truck," said Lillian. "None of those is him."

"No," said Lester.

"He's not here," said Lillian.

"Probably he ain't," said Lester. "Maybe that Murdock fellow is."

Nate turned off the truck's engine. He opened his door.

"No," said Lester. "I'll scope it out. You wait here."

Lester left the truck, walked to the Fort, opened the door, and went in. As he did, two men came out of the place. They made their way to two of the motorcycles parked in front of the Fort, and mounted. They mounted, not without effort. These motorcyclists were not like the motorcyclists of former times, youthful, dashing, riding always on the edge of violence. These riders had stepped back from that edge some time ago. They were riders of a lesser breed, a degenerate breed: slowed-down, shaggy, grizzled, like middle-aged wolves who have retired to the zoo — a little beat-up, a little overweight. They climbed onto their machines, started them, and rumbled through the parking lot to the road, where they made off in a snarl from their engines, spitting gravel.

Lillian watched them. Were those two friends of Blackway? They were old. They could barely get onto their bikes. How tough could they be? Did Lester and Nate know what they were doing, after all?

"Are they friends of Blackway's?" she asked Nate.

"Who?"

"The two who just left."

"Don't know," said Nate. "Maybe."

"They don't look so tough, do they? You could handle them."

"'Course I could. What do you think?"

"But then, they aren't Blackway."

"I ain't scared of Blackway," said Nate.

Lillian looked at him. Nate's head nearly touched the truck cab's roof as he sat behind the wheel, his shoulders spanned more than half the cab, or they seemed to, and his right arm, resting on the seat beside her, looked like a wooden beam. He was big enough. Maybe Nate wasn't bright. Maybe he could hardly talk. But he certainly was big enough.

Lester came out of the Fort, crossed to the truck, and stood by the passenger's window.

"Well," he said, "there's more in there than I could have wanted, but we'll be all right, I guess."

"Blackway?" Lillian asked.

"No," Lester said.

"The other one?" asked Lillian. "Murdock?"

"He's there," Lester said.

"He don't scare me," said Nate. "I'm ready." He laced his fingers together in front of him and cracked his knuckles. "Let's go," he said.

"Hold it," said Lester. "Just hold it a minute. No fists. You understand? You be ready if we have to get into it with him. But I don't want to see no fists. This ain't the Olympics, you know. It ain't a boxing match. You have to hit a man, hit him *with* something. Not your fist, something hard. That way, you only have to hit him once."

"I ain't scared of him, I told you," said Nate.

"'Course you ain't," said Lester. "But that don't mean you have to pat him on the head like a puppy. You want to finish it quick, before it starts. That's the best way. This guy in there, you know the kind of guy he is: big, heavy fellow, got the black beard, the shaved head, the black leather suit. He wants to scare you to death. He wants to scare you to death because he knows if he don't, he's in trouble. He won't take hitting — him especially, I'm guessing."

"What does that mean?" Lillian asked.

"We'll have to see," said Lester. "I'm guessing he looks a lot worse than he is."

"He'd have to, it sounds like, wouldn't he?"

"You got that right, too."

"Why don't you fight him, then?"

"My fighting days are done," Lester said. "But I taught this kid everything I know."

"You did?"

"'Course I did."

"Is that right?" Lillian asked Nate.

Nate shrugged.

"'Course it's right," said Lester.

"Are we doing this?" asked Nate.

Nate opened his door and left the truck. He stood to his full height and stretched his back, then his neck, then his arms, letting them hang down like heavy cables from his shoulders and shaking them. He waited for Lester and Lillian. Lillian got out of the car, and the three of them, first Nate, then Lillian, then Lester, went into the Fort.

12

SYMPOSIUM

Coop went to the window.

"Here's Scotty," he said.

"Did he bring the beer?" Whizzer asked him.

"He brought something," said Coop.

They heard his steps on the board floor outside, and then Scott Cavanaugh came into the office with a case of Ballantines under his arm. He set it on the desk between Whizzer and Conrad.

"Afternoon, girls," said Cavanaugh.

"Where have you been?" Whizzer asked him. "We're about dried out, here." He shoved the case across the desk toward Conrad.

"White River," said Cavanaugh. "Seeing Arthur and them."

"How's their little girl doing?" Coop asked.

"Not real well," Cavanaugh said. "They're saying another round of the chemo. She looks okay. Got hair again. Gritting it out. She's doing better than they are."

Whizzer shook his head. "You want to hand that out, there?" he asked Conrad.

"Oh," said Conrad. "Sure." He stood, opened the case of beer, and passed the cold cans around among them. They opened their beers: five tiny explosions.

"You know Con," Whizzer said to Cavanaugh.

"Sure," said Cavanaugh. "How are you doing?"

"Thanks for the beer," said Conrad.

"Don't thank me," said Cavanaugh. "Whiz said bring it. I brought it."

"We've been telling Con about that time you and Blackway had your little disagreement at the Fort," said Whizzer.

"Your little difference of opinion," said D.B.

"I seem to recall," said Cavanaugh.

"I bet you do," said Coop. "We were trying to remember what was it he hit Cal with, that time? Whiz says a bar, but it wasn't a bar. It was a chair, wasn't it? He hit him with a chair."

"I'm not exactly sure," said Cavanaugh.

"'Course he ain't," Whizzer told Coop.

"Out cold, weren't you?" D.B. asked Cavanaugh.

"Hell, no," Cavanaugh said. "He never knocked me out. And I had my shot at him, too. Don't worry about that. I hurt him."

"Is that right?" Whizzer asked.

"When was that?" Coop asked.

"Just before," Cavanaugh said. "He swung on me. I ducked it and got one into his middle. Broke a rib, I think. I felt something let go, anyway."

"Sure, you did," said Coop.

"Couldn't have been hurt too bad, though, I guess," said Whizzer, "since he came right back and put you out for, what? A week, was it?"

"My foot slipped," Cavanaugh said. "I fell into it, his shot. Otherwise it would have been different. Don't worry, though: I hurt him. Don't worry about that."

"Sure, you did," said Coop.

"We had somebody in here, before," said Whizzer. "Looking for you."

"A girl," said D.B.

Cavanaugh grinned. "You did?" he asked. "Another one?"

"Kevin's girl, it was," said Coop. "The one used to be Kevin's."

Cavanaugh put down his beer.

"Kevin's girl?" he asked.

"Same one," said Coop.

"What do you mean, you had her here?" Cavanaugh asked.

"She was here," Whizzer said. "What did you think?"

"What do you mean, before?" Cavanaugh asked.

"This morning bright and early," Coop said.

"She was here?" Cavanaugh asked.

"What we've been telling you, ain't it?" Whizzer asked.

"Why?" Cavanaugh asked.

"Looking for you," Coop said.

"Looking for you for help with Blackway," said D.B.

"Help?" Cavanaugh asked.

"He's been after her," Coop said.

"Following her," D.B. said.

"Stalking her," Coop said.

"Bashed in her window," D.B. said.

"Killed her cat," Coop said.

"Jesus," Cavanaugh said.

"She went to Wingate," Coop said.

"Wingate told her there was nothing he could do," said Whizzer.

"'Course there wasn't," said Coop. "There's never nothing Wingate can do, is there?"

"Wingate told her to find you," Whizzer went on. "Told her you'd help her out."

"Jesus," said Cavanaugh. "Help her, how?"

"That wasn't too clear," said Conrad.

"Take Blackway down for her, it looks like," said D.B.

"Like you did that time," said Coop.

"That time your foot slipped," said D.B.

"This is Russell's kid's girlfriend, right?" Cavanaugh asked. "Kevin's girlfriend? The skinny one with the hair?"

"That's the one," said D.B.

"She ain't either skinny," said Whizzer.

"Whiz likes her," Coop told Cavanaugh.

"She was here," said Cavanaugh. "So, where is she now?"

"You weren't around," said Whizzer. "She went along."

"With Les and Nate the Great," said Coop.

"Les?" asked Cavanaugh. "Les Speed?"

"Les and the kid," said Whizzer. "Nate the Great."

"She went with them?" Cavanaugh asked. "What for?"

"They're going to take care of it for her," said Whizzer.

"Take care of Blackway?" Cavanaugh asked.

"We told her," said Coop.

"Warned her," said D.B.

"Told her she didn't want to get into something with Blackway. She ought to just leave town," said Coop.

"She wouldn't do it," said Whizzer. "Won't run, she said."

"Some pistol," said D.B.

"Blackway might have picked on the wrong girl, this time, it looks like," said Whizzer.

"They went off after him," said Coop.

"Her and Les and Nate the Great," said D.B.

Cavanaugh laughed. "This is a joke, right?" he asked.

"No joke," said Whizzer.

"They went with her," said D.B.

"To find Blackway," said Whizzer.

"You wouldn't know where he is, would you?" Coop asked.

"Les Speed and Nate are going up against Blackway?" Cavanaugh said.

"It looks that way," said Coop.

"They haven't got a chance," said Cavanaugh. "Blackway will eat them alive."

"That's what the girl said," said Whizzer.

"She said the same thing," said Coop.

"Plus," said Cavanaugh, "what about his friends? The others they got to go through before they get to Blackway? What about them?"

"They know about them," said Coop.

"Les reckons they can handle them," said Whizzer.

"He reckons wrong," said Cavanaugh.

"Maybe," said Whizzer. "They went ahead anyway."

"When?" asked Cavanaugh.

"Oh, couple of hours ago," said Whizzer. "Three?"

"Four?" Coop said.

Cavanaugh got to his feet. "I've got to go," he said.

"Oh, come on," said D.B.

"Finish your beer," said Whizzer.

"Have another," said Coop.

"Take one for the drive," said D.B.

But Cavanaugh wouldn't wait. He nodded to them and left the office, leaving his unfinished beer on the floor.

"Where's he going?" D.B. asked.

"Is he going after the others?" Conrad asked.

"Likely he's not," said Coop.

"Likely he's headed the other way," said Whizzer.

"Headed for someplace else," said Coop.

"Someplace like Australia," said Whizzer.

13

MURDOCK'S EAR

Seven people seemed to be in the Fort that afternoon — the bar-tender and six drinkers: two at the bar, three at tables, one in a booth along the wall. The bartender was talking to one of the men at the bar, but the other man there, and the three at tables, were alone. The room was quiet. It usually was. The Fort had never been much of a party shop.

For a moment after they entered, Lillian couldn't see because of the dark. She waited inside the door, peering. She saw Lester go to the bar, with Nate following him. Lester ordered a large pitcher of beer and took it, with three glasses, from the bar to the booth in the corner, where the man was sitting by himself. Lester set the pitcher and glasses on the table in the booth and pulled a chair over to the end of the table, with the booth's occupant, Murdock, to his left. Lester sat. Nate remained standing.

Lillian saw Lester beckon to her. She left the door and crossed the room to the booth where the three men waited.

Nate let Lillian slide into the booth and then sat beside her, opposite Murdock. Murdock hadn't spoken. He was looking from Lester to Nate. Lester nodded toward the pitcher of beer on the table before him.

"Buy you a beer," he said to Murdock.

"I know you?" Murdock asked.

Even sitting in the booth, Murdock looked like a big man. His upper body bent over the little table before him like a leaning tower, and his knees crowded in beneath it. He was as tall as Nate and far heavier. Lillian watched him. Murdock was very still. He waited. He didn't know what Lester's play was. But he didn't seem watchful or wary. He seemed amused, he seemed tickled by the old woodchuck, the big young kid, and the silent girl with them.

Lester reached for the beer pitcher and motioned with it toward Murdock's glass. "On us," he told Murdock.

"You're fucking-A right it's on you," said Murdock. "I didn't ask you to come over here. What do you want?"

Lester raised the pitcher and poured a quick glass, less than full, for each of them and Murdock. He set the pitcher, still three-quarters full, on the table to his right.

Murdock looked at his glass.

"Jesus," he said, "what are you saving it for? Pour it out."

"Plenty of time," said Lester.

"For what?" Murdock asked.

"Well," said Lester, "we're looking for Blackway."

"Blackway?" said Murdock. "Who's Blackway?"

Lester laughed. "We went by the High Line," he said. "They said he might be here."

"You see he ain't," said Murdock.

"Maybe he's at his place up in the Towns?" Lester asked.

"Maybe he is," said Murdock. "Maybe he ain't. Why? What do you want with Blackway?"

Lillian looked from Lester to Murdock as they went back and forth. She waited for Lester and Nate to start a routine about why they were looking for Blackway, but Lester only said, "He's been making trouble for the lady."

"Lady?" Murdock asked. "You mean her? I heard about her. Blackway's fucking her. She's your idea of a lady?"

"He ain't, either," said Nate. Lester gave him a sharp look, but Murdock went on.

"If he ain't, he will be," said Murdock. "Listen: Blackway gets what he wants. He wants her, he's got her. She wouldn't be the first. She won't be the last."

"No?" said Lester.

"No," said Murdock. "I seen all kinds of Blackway's ladies. *Ladies.*" He leaned forward and spat on the table between him and Lillian. Nate began to move to his left to get out of the booth, but Lester put his hand on his arm to stop him. Nate sat back, watching Murdock.

Lester chuckled. "Well," he said, "there's ladies and ladies. You and Blackway know each other pretty well, I guess."

Murdock didn't answer him. He drank his beer.

"Go back a long way, I guess," Lester said.

"We do," said Murdock.

"'Course, it's got to be tough, too," said Lester. "Coming from where you've been."

"Where I've been?"

"Well, you know," said Lester. "You know: the place?"

Murdock looked at Lester for a moment. His eyes grew wide. Then he shook his head and seemed almost to smile. "You know who you're talking to?" he asked.

"Has to be tough," Lester went on. "In the place. All the stuff goes on in there. Then you get out, you go looking for your friends. What do you find?"

"What?" Murdock asked him.

But Lester only shook his head sympathetically and drained his glass of beer. "We heard Blackway's up in the Towns," said Lester. "If he is, up there, would he be alone, about now?"

"How would I know?" said Murdock.

Lester nodded. "Well, then," he said, but he made no move to leave his seat at the end of the table. Instead he reached for the beer pitcher and got ready to give himself another round.

"Why don't you ask her?" Murdock said. "Don't ask me. Ask her. Your lady. Ask the lady where Blackway is. He's fucking her, ain't he? It's her Blackway's fucking, it ain't me."

Lester chuckled again.

"Ain't it?" Lester asked.

Murdock, who had been looking at Lillian, slowly blinked his eyes one time. He turned to Lester.

"What was that?" he asked.

Nate moved again to leave the booth.

"What was that you just said?" Murdock asked Lester.

Nate was on his feet. Murdock turned toward him, struggling to get out of the booth, bumping the table with his knees as he tried to rise. Lillian looked from one to the other of them, but it was Lester she should have been watching.

Still sitting at the end of the table, Lester picked up the nearly full beer pitcher by its handle and swung it up off the table and around behind him to his right. A little beer spilled on the table. Lester brought the heavy glass pitcher around in a long sidearm arc, accelerating, and landed it on the left side of Murdock's head. The pitcher exploded with a loud, hollow bang, and a pink plume of glass, foam, beer, and blood sprayed over the back of the booth, the floor, and the nearby tables.

"Go," said Lester to Nate. "Go ahead, now."

Nate pulled Lillian out of the booth and steered her across the room toward the exit. Nobody tried to stop them. The men at the bar hadn't moved. The men at the tables hadn't moved. The bartender had disappeared.

At the door with Nate, Lillian looked back for Lester. He was still at the booth. Murdock had been knocked partly out of the booth and lay half on the seat, half on the floor beside the booth. He was unconscious if he wasn't dead, and Lillian could see blood covering the side of his face and running freely onto the floor. Lillian saw Lester take Murdock by the back of his collar and drag him out of the booth. He dumped Murdock onto the floor and stood over him. Lillian watched Lester raise his foot and drive his boot down onto Murdock's knee, jumping on it with all his weight. The bone gave, making a pop that Lillian could hear as Nate hurried her out the door — the last thing she heard that afternoon at Fort Bob.

Nate started the engine. Lester came out of the Fort and got in beside Lillian. They drove out of the parking lot and onto the road.

"You killed that guy," said Lillian.

"You mean Murdock?" Lester said. "'Course I didn't. He'll be fine. Might need a few stitches."

"Fine?" said Lillian. "There was blood all over the room."

"I was ready to take him," Nate said, "soon as I got clear of that table."

"I know you were," said Lester. "I could see you were getting ready for him."

"I saw you stomp on him," Lillian told Lester. "I saw you do that. He was down. Why did you have to smash his leg?"

"You wouldn't have done that, I guess?" Lester said.

"He was on the floor," said Lillian. "He was out of it."

"I guess you'd rather he'd get up off the floor and come after us," said Lester. "I fixed it so that won't happen."

Lillian was silent.

"You wanted a fight," said Lester. "You got one."

"I didn't want that," said Lillian. "I saw him lying on the floor. I saw the blood. If you didn't kill him, you came close. And you're telling me he'll be good as new?"

"Not quite," said Lester. "Look here."

He held out on the palm of his hand a brown, flat object that might have been a cookie — held it out toward Nate and Lillian.

"Look at that," said Lester.

"What is it?" Lillian asked. "Oh," she said.

Lester was showing them Murdock's left ear, or at any rate most of it; some of the lobe hadn't come away with the rest.

"It got thrown clear across the room, you know?" Lester told them. "I picked it up off the floor going out."

"Oh," said Lillian.

"That's a clean cut," said Lester.

"What are we going to do with it?" Nate asked.

"I guess we could give it back to Murdock," said Lester. "You want to?" he asked Lillian.

Lillian shook her head.

"I guess not," said Lester, and he flicked his wrist and sailed the severed ear out the window. "Left up here," he told Nate.

"Where are we going?" Lillian asked.

"Where everybody's been telling us to go," said Lester. "The Towns."

14

THE LOST TOWNS

Loggers, hunters, campers, hikers had gone into the Lost Towns and never been seen again. More than a few, over the years. Ten or twelve men and women had simply disappeared up there.

It wouldn't have been hard to do. The Towns were a big piece of real estate: a hundred square miles of nothing but woods, ravines, beaver ponds, and silent little brooks that made their hidden ways under the dark and tangled branches of the firs. In the entire tract, there was one road, no village, no structure bigger than a hunting camp and no more than two or three of those.

The district took in the whole of two townships and parts of five others. At one time there had been some settlement in the principal towns, there had been a few farms, but they had been given up decades, generations since. The populations of those two towns today stood, the one at two, the other at zero; and as for who exactly the two might be and where exactly they might dwell, nobody knew.

The only livelihood that had endured in the Lost Towns was the timber business. If you made your living from trees, then you still had a use for the Towns. Loggers had cut their way through the area time and time again, leaving trails and tracks that wound over the hills, going this way and that, going nowhere, soon vanishing in the returning forest.

That forest, green, shadowed, quickly claimed and reclaimed everything in the Towns, every foot of them, except here and there where the timber companies had made more permanent marks in the form of vast sawmill tailings or piles. The bigger operators would set up camp in the woods and bring in their own mill to saw the logs on the spot. When these camps got done with their work, and were broken down and taken away, they left behind them brown and yellow hills, beaches, dunes of sawdust in which nothing could grow. Those sawdust wastes, some of them decades old and several acres in extent, were left here and there throughout the Towns like pocket deserts of infertility, sunbaked amid the vast green surround.

It was at one of those sawdust deserts, or near it, that the Lost Towns' best remembered and least explained disappearance had occurred. The timber company, owned at the time by Fitzgerald's father, had had a crew of choppers up in the heart of the Towns since January: four men from Quebec and a log skidder. Sometime in early April one of the company's scalers had hiked in on snowshoes to rate their cut. The four had been living in a kind of cabin in the woods, put up out of two-by-fours, plywood, and tar paper, that the company had provided as a bunkhouse. The scaler found the cabin, he found the men's clothes and other gear, their supplies. He found dried-out food on the table. He found the skidder parked nearby. But of the four Frenchmen he found no trace, nor did anybody else, ever.

State police, officers of the fish and game department, and volunteers from the timber company went over the area looking for any sign of the missing men or of what had become of them, but they didn't keep at it very long. The police had brought a dog handler with them. His dogs, a pair of bloodhounds, could do nothing, and their owner absolutely refused to keep them in the Towns overnight. The other searchers didn't argue with him. If you find a French chopper, then a French chopper is all you've found; but if in the process you lose a bloodhound, then you've lost a valuable animal.

"Great big things," Lester said. "Bigger than a shepherd. And crazy for the scent, just crazy for it. You ever seen one of those dogs work?"

"What dogs?" said Nate.

Lester had been with the timber company's men looking for the loggers that early-spring day in the Towns.

"They cast all around," he said. "'Cast,' they call it. They're looking for a scent line. They're strong. They about pulled the guy off his feet."

"What happened?" Lillian asked. "What did they find?"

"Nothing," said Lester. "They found nothing."

"Come on," said Lillian.

"I'm telling you," said Lester. "I was there. They reckoned nobody had been in the camp for at least three, four weeks, might have been more. And it was still winter up there. April? There must have been a couple, three feet of snow on the ground."

"Well, then, they left," said Lillian. "Didn't they?"

"They didn't leave," said Lester.

"Come on," said Lillian. "What are you saying? Are you saying somebody came in and did something to them? That's a fairy tale."

"A fairy tale?" said Lester. "Well, maybe it is a fairy tale. I'll tell you one thing, though: If somebody did come in and took on those choppers, it was no fairy. Whoever did that had to been made of some serious stuff. Those French guys were no joke. None of them was much over five feet high, but tough? Didn't speak a word of English, jabbered away at each other all day long, they never shut up. But they knew how to work, and they knew how to fight. Fight's what they did when they weren't working: fight with themselves. They arm wrestled, fought with their fists, their feet, sticks, even knives, even axes. They'd fight with their god damned axes. They were all crazy. The company used to bring them down every year from Canada."

"They went home," said Lillian.

"And left all their stuff?" Lester asked her. "Their clothes? Never got paid? Besides, the cops asked. Their people, where they came from, never saw them. The company ended up paying their families — oh, I don't remember — five thousand, was it? A lot, at the time. Fitz's old man was pissed."

"Okay," said Lillian. "What do you think happened to them, then?"

"I don't know," said Lester. "You don't know what happened up there. But I don't rule nothing out. The Towns are a funny old place. You're a long way off the road up there."

"Fairy tales," said Lillian.

"Pull it over up ahead," Lester said to Nate.

They had left the highway and gone north on the road that went into the Lost Towns. For three or four miles it was a good road, then it wasn't. They bumped hard across washouts, in and out of holes, over rocks. At last Nate brought the truck into a turnout and parked. The four of them sat. All around them were woods full of the midafternoon light and shadow, dense woods that didn't let you see more than a few yards into them. So quiet: no birdcalls, no noise. The only sound was from an airplane passing somewhere high overhead — that, and the ticking of the truck's engine as it cooled.

For a minute none of them spoke. Then Lillian asked, "How far is Blackway's?"

"Another mile, two miles, on this," said Lester. "Then there's a log road goes left, up the mountain. Another mile on that."

"Walking?" Lillian asked.

"That's right," said Lester.

"Why?" Lillian asked. "Can't we make it in this?"

"We could, you know it?" Nate said to Lester.

"We could," said Lester. "We could get as far as the log road, probably. Everybody could know about it, too. You can hear a vehicle a mile away up here. We don't need that. We'll walk from here."

"Three miles?" said Lillian. "It'll be dark before we get to Blackway's."

"Probably it will," said Lester.

"You don't care?" asked Lillian. "You won't be able to see what you're doing. Will you?"

"Neither will Blackway," said Lester.

"What's he want up there, anyway?" Conrad asked.

"Blackway?" said Coop. "Blackway likes it up there. It's quiet up there — in the Towns."

"Nothing up there but bears and moose and birds," said D.B.

"Them and whatever it was got all those people," said Whizzer.

"What people?" Conrad asked.

"Nothing got them," said Coop. "They got lost. They died in the woods. Anything else is a crock."

"Who got lost?" Conrad asked.

"You've been up there," Coop went on. "You know what it's

like. Those woods. You get fifty feet off the trail and you can't see a god damned thing. You don't know where you are. You get turned around, you'll never find your way out. It ain't like down here, where you'll always come to somebody's line, somebody's fence, some brook you can follow down to the road. Up there, there ain't no lines, there ain't no fences. The brooks don't go no place. The thing is, there's nothing up there. Those people didn't understand that. They got lost and they never got found. That's all that happened."

"Well," said Whizzer, "maybe that's so for that college girl, maybe for the bird-watchers, even the hunters. But are you going to say those four choppers got lost? They lived in there."

"What college girl?" Conrad asked.

"Oh, few years ago," said Whizzer. "Girl was in college over there in Bennington. Told her friends she was going to drive up into the Towns. Camp out, I guess."

"Get back to Nature," said Coop.

"A Bennington girl?" Conrad asked. "It can't be."

"She didn't come back," Whizzer went on. "Next day, her friends went up there looking for her. Nothing."

"They found her car," said D.B.

"They sure didn't," said Whizzer. "They found nothing."

"They found her car, Whiz," said D.B. "Remember? They had to get a wrecker in there and tow it out. It sat outside the garage there in Searsburg for years. It might still be there."

"That was Mackenzie's car they towed out of there, that other time, when he threw the rod," said Whizzer, "not the college girl's."

"Another college girl," said D.B.

"What do you mean, another?" Whizzer asked him.

"Like What's-her-name," said D.B. "Goes around, thinks she's something special. Gets jammed up."

"This one's no college girl," said Whizzer. "Our girl ain't."

"Ain't she?" D.B. asked. "She thinks she is. Acts like she is. Her and her *You people*. Thinks she's something."

"Still," said Whizzer, "she ain't no college girl. I told you that before."

"Con's a college man," said D.B. "What do you say?" he asked Conrad. "She look like a college girl to you?"

"Probably not," said Conrad.

"See, there?" said Whizzer. "What did I say?"

"Hard to tell sometimes, though," said Conrad.

"Point is," said Coop. "Nobody ever heard from the girl again. The other one. She just disappeared up there."

"Somebody said she took off because she was in trouble," said D.B. "She was getting ready to have the wrong guy's kid."

"For that she vanishes into the wilderness?" Conrad asked. "Because she's knocked up? Because she's been screwing around? A Bennington girl? Come on. I'm a college man, you know. My sister went to Bennington. At Bennington for screwing around you get Phi Beta Kappa."

"What's Phi Beta Kappa?" asked D.B.

From the turnout where they had left the truck, a trail, two wheel ruts with wild grasses growing waist-high between them, went sharply uphill. To either side, in the brush growth, hardhack lifted its fuzzy flowers like pink tapers, and wild blackberries reached for them with their barbed canes. The three walked in single file: first Nate, then Lillian, then Lester, limping along in the rear carrying his parcel snug under his right arm. Little orange butterflies skipped back and forth across the track in front of them, like ragged children running in front of a procession, and overhead a hawk or some other such bird sailed high above them in the blue, its wings unmoving, rising and falling lazily on the wind that passed over the mountain's side and breathed faintly in the thick woods around them.

They weren't the first to have come up this way recently. The grass in the center of the track was knocked down flat, and here and there they passed a rock in one of the ruts with a black graze of rubber on it, or they saw a place where a heavy tire had come down and printed its tread into the bare dirt.

Lillian watched Nate walking in front of her. Nate walked with his head down, staring at the ground before him. His strides were long and heavy; his shoulders rose and fell. Nate wore a dirty gray T-shirt that was printed across the back in blue letters: S.T.U.D.

"What's S.T.U.D.?" Lillian asked.

Lester snorted from the rear, but Nate walked on without answering.

"Hey, Nate?" Lillian asked.

"Yo."

"What's S.T.U.D.?"

"What?"

"S.T.U.D.," Lillian said. "Your shirt."

"What about it?"

"Well," Lillian asked, "what is it? What does it mean?"

"What do you think it means?" Lester asked her from behind.

"It don't mean nothing," said Nate. "They were giving them away."

"Don't believe him," said Lester. "His girlfriend gave it to him. Didn't she, Nate? That Rowena gave it to you, didn't she?"

"No," said Nate.

"Rowena?" asked Lillian.

"Works at the clinic," said Lester. "She's a nurse, ain't she? Ain't she some kind of a nurse?"

"She's a technician," said Nate.

"I'll bet she is," said Lester.

"What?" said Nate.

"Gave the boy that S.T.U.D. shirt for his birthday," said Lester. "You know why."

"She didn't," said Nate. "They were giving them away."

"She was, anyway," said Lester.

"What?" said Nate.

"Nothing," said Lester.

"She ain't my girlfriend," said Nate.

Lillian walked on. She watched Nate. She watched the T-shirt stretch across his shoulders and over the muscle in his back. It wasn't a bad-looking back, come to it. Come to it, Nate wasn't bad-looking goods. Not at all. Not from the back. But Rowena? What kind of a name was Rowena, anyway? It was a woodchuck name. It was a name like Tiffany or Brittney — the name of a girl who marries a guy with a large back. A back like Nate's. She marries a guy like Nate. He marries her. They live in East Schmuckville. What would Kevin have had to say about them? She could hear Kevin. She could hear Kevin talking about Nate and Rowena. She could hear Kevin's contempt. But Kevin was gone, wasn't he?

"She ain't either my girlfriend," said Nate, walking ahead.

———

"Like you say, 'into the wilderness'?" said Coop. "That ain't wilderness. The Towns ain't wilderness like you've got in Maine, Canada, out West."

"Well," said Whizzer, "but this ain't out West. Here, if the Towns ain't wilderness, they'll do until the real thing comes along."

"Which it won't," said Coop.

"Won't what?" D.B. asked him.

"You know," said Coop. "The woods. The Towns. They ain't coming, they're going. They're going now. People moving in, clearing, building. Roads and what have you. It's all going away."

"Not in the Towns," said D.B. "That's all government land, up there."

"There, too," said Coop. "Government land? So what if it is? The government bought it, the government can sell it. If people want that land, they'll have it. The government can't stop them."

"They are the government," said Conrad.

"There you go," said Coop. "Someday that will be like the suburbs up there: little streets, little houses."

"Lawns," said Whizzer. "Guys out after work, cutting the grass."

"Schools," said Coop.

"Wal-Mart," said Conrad. "Colonel Sanders."

"Taco Bell," said D.B.

"Bars," said Coop. "You can stop off for a beer."

"Don't sound so bad, at that, does it?" said Whizzer.

Nate turned back to look for Lester. He pointed up the trail ahead of them. There, visible through the green woods, a shining, a flashing — something bright.

Lester came from the rear and signaled to Lillian and Nate to stay where they were. Then he went forward toward the bright object. The track took a bend, and Lester disappeared around it, into the trees.

Lillian went to a boulder beside the trail and rested against it.

"Nate?" she asked.

"Yo," said Nate.

"What's the plan, here?"

"What?"

"What's the plan, for Blackway?" asked Lillian. "Your and Lester's plan, for when we find him?"

"Plan?"

"That's right. Like with the others — Murdock, the rest of them. You've got a plan, right?"

"I ain't afraid of Blackway," said Nate.

"No, but Lester," said Lillian. "He's got a plan, doesn't he? With the gun he's got? Something?"

"Thought you didn't want no guns in this," said Nate. "Before, you didn't want no guns."

"Look," said Lillian. "What I want is for this to be over with. I want you — I want us — to take care of Blackway. I want to know how that's going to happen."

"Well," said Nate, "all I know is I ain't afraid of Blackway."

Lester came back around the bend. "Come ahead," he said. Lillian pushed herself up off her seat and followed Nate.

A big Ford pickup truck was parked beside the trail. It was fairly new, black, with the body cranked up high off its axles atop over-sized tires.

"That's Blackway's," said Lillian.

Nate was beside the truck, looking into the driver's-side window.

"Keys are in it," he said.

"He forgot the keys?" Lillian asked.

"He didn't forget them," Lester said. "He left them. Why not? Anybody who knows whose truck this is ain't about to steal it."

"What if they don't know whose it is?" Lillian asked.

"They know," said Lester. "If they're up here, they know." To Nate he said, "Go ahead."

Nate opened the truck's door and took the keys from the ignition. He tossed them over the hood to Lester. Lester caught the keys and held them up, showing them to Lillian.

"You understand," Lester said. He was speaking to both of them. "You understand we're about down on it, now." He jingled the keys. "If we take Blackway's keys, here — what I mean, once we take them, he's stuck, but so are we. We can't turn this thing around. If we do this, we got to finish it. We got to go through. You see that."

"I do," said Lillian.

"I ain't afraid of Blackway," said Nate.

15

GOING THROUGH

"Beer's by you, ain't it?" Whizzer said to Conrad.

"It is," said Conrad. He reached into the case and brought forth four more cans.

D.B. opened his beer, drank, belched.

"All right," he said. "You were talking about the Towns? All right, you can argue about whether to call it wilderness up there and how much longer you're going to be able to call it whatever you decide to call it. Point is, now, today, that's still wild country, the Towns."

"A man can be free up there," said Coop.

"Blackway thinks so," said Whizzer.

"No women," said D.B.

"No kids," said Coop.

"No traffic," said D.B.

"No phones," said Coop.

"No cops," said Whizzer.

"No cops?" said Conrad. "What about Wingate?"

"What about him?" asked Coop.

"Wingate's sheriff," said Whizzer. "Sheriff's a county officer. The Towns are over the line."

"Sheriff's office can go in there if they have to, though," said D.B.

"Not by law, they can't," said Whizzer.

"Not by law," said Coop. "Whiz is right. By law, the Towns are out of Wingate's beat. By law, they are. And we all know how Wingate feels about the law."

"Here we go," said Whizzer.

"We all know," Coop went on, "how Wingate will ride the law even when it don't make sense to ride it, even when the law ain't what it's all about. Like with that girl and Blackway."

"That wasn't about the law?" Whizzer asked him.

"No," said Coop. "It wasn't. The law ain't what What's-her-name needed. She needed help. Wingate and his law blew her off. Where is she now?"

"Don't know," said D.B. "Do you?"

"Listen," said Whizzer. "Wingate knows what he's doing. He knew she needed help. She told him. If he didn't go to help her himself, it was because he had a better plan."

"Right," said Coop. "Scotty Cavanaugh. Scotty was a hell of a plan of Wingate's, wasn't he?"

"Well," said Whizzer. "Where's Scotty now?"

"Far away as he can get," said Coop.

"So, what do you make of that?" Whizzer asked him.

"Nothing," said Coop. "I don't make nothing of it. Wingate didn't know Scotty wouldn't be going with her. He didn't know Scotty wouldn't be here."

"Didn't he?" said Whizzer.

Lester stopped. "We're getting close," he said. "You two wait here a minute. I'll go on up to the corner there and take a little look."

He went ahead up the track, carrying his parcel under his arm. He disappeared around a bend. Lillian and Nate stood in the trail. The long afternoon quickened its pace as the sun, white, then yellow, then gold, fell steadily toward the hills. Now the dips in the trail were in shadow.

Lillian sat down in the grass beside the trail. Nate stood. He looked down at Lillian, looked away. He was bouncing gently on the balls of his feet, pacing, restless. They had walked three miles over broken ground, and Nate couldn't stand still. Lillian was all in. Her side hurt, her ankles hurt. Her clothes stuck to her. She pushed her damp hair back behind her ears with her fingers. She looked up at Nate.

"Take it easy," said Lillian. "Rest. What's the matter with you?"

"Who?"

"You. Dancing around. Relax. Here, sit down." Lillian patted the ground beside her.

"I'll stand," said Nate.

Lillian looked up at him. "Rowena, huh?" she asked. "Rowena what?"

"She ain't my girlfriend," said Nate.

"Lester thinks she is."

"Les don't know everything."

"What's her last name?"

"Whose?"

"Rowena's."

"Pinto," said Nate.

"Rowena Pinto," said Lillian. "Are you going to get married?"

"Who?"

Lillian shook her head. She kept on shaking it. She began to laugh. She began, and then she couldn't stop.

"What's the matter?" Nate asked her.

"Nothing," said Lillian. She went on laughing.

"Yeah, well, cut it out," said Nate. "You sound like that one at the High Line."

"I know," she said. "I know I do."

"Come on, now," said Nate.

Gasping, Lillian let her laughter trickle away. It ran out of her like the last water runs out of a drain. This was not going to work.

"This isn't going to work, is it?" Lillian said.

"What?" asked Nate.

Lilllian shook her head. Blackway rose before her like a dark wall, he watched her. He broke Kevin like a pencil. He blew Kevin out like a birthday candle. He erased him. What had Kevin looked like? Lillian couldn't remember. Blackway filled the rear of her little car with shattered glass, he caught her little cat in his hands and held her as she struggled. He took what he wanted, he did what he wanted. Nobody could stop him. Nate was big, but size wasn't enough. And anyway, Nate belonged to Rowena Pinto, didn't he? Nate and Rowena would marry. Of course they would. They weren't like her. They would marry and start making babies, and all of them would be boys, every one of them; even the girls would be boys. You couldn't get away from it. You couldn't. If you tried, there was Blackway. Tears stood on Lillian's cheeks. She brushed them away with her fingers.

"Are you okay?" Nate was asking her.

Lillian sniffed. She had stopped laughing, she had stopped crying. "I'm okay," she said.

"Here's Les," said Nate.

Lillian looked up the trail where Lester came around the bend and approached them. He was limping worse than he had been earlier, and he leaned on a branch he had cut for a staff. Lillian watched him. Nate and Rowena's boys would grow up and get old and soon they would be all shot. They would be like Lester and like the broken-down, cackling old clowns who sat around the mill all day, cracking one another up, and farting, and scratching their useless crotches. They didn't like her. They didn't like her hair, they didn't like her mouth. They didn't like anything about her. They had sent her out here with a sixth-grade dropout and a senior citizen who could hardly walk. They wouldn't be her protectors, even if they could. None of them would. This thing was not going to work.

"I'm okay," Lillian said again.

"Come on, Whiz," said Coop. "You're telling me Wingate had this whole thing down? He knew Scotty wasn't going to be here when that girl came? He knew Les and Nate were? He knew you'd have them go with her?"

"You said it," said Whizzer. "Not me."

"You don't believe that," said Coop.

"Don't I?" said Whizzer. "Well, maybe I don't. Maybe I do. But I'll tell you something else: Wingate knows plenty. You fellows don't give Wingate much credit. He's not so dumb."

"Ain't he?" asked Coop. "He fooled me."

"Maybe he did, at that," said Whizzer. "You wouldn't be the first. You ever played cards with Wingate?"

"Cards?" Coop asked.

"This young fellow remembers," Whizzer said, grinning at D.B. "Don't you?"

D.B. was chuckling and shaking his head. "Like it was yesterday," he said. "Like it was this morning. I never did know what that was all about, though, did you? Did Wingate really have that thing fixed?"

"You can take it to the bank," said Whizzer.

"Have what thing fixed?" Conrad asked.

Lester beckoned to them. "Come ahead," he said. "It's right around the corner."

"What is?" Lillian asked.

"Blackway's," said Lester.

"Is he there?" Lillian asked.

"Nobody's there," Lester said.

"Listen, Lester —" Lillian began. Lester didn't hear.

"We'll wait for him," said Lester. "It works fine. I'd rather him walk in on us than us on him. Come ahead."

"Wait a minute," said Lillian. But Lester had turned off the trail with Nate following. Lillian had no choice. She went after them.

Past the bend, the trail ran downhill into a shallow bowl in the mountains. On the right, the woods; on the left, a large barren, one of the old sawmill tailings, covering a couple of acres with a desert of packed sawdust: brown, hot, drifted into peaks and hummocks, practically void of growth except for a few weeds, a few tough dry stalks that hung on here and there, stirring in the little wind that passed over the waste.

"What's this?" Lillian asked.

"This was Boyd's Job," said Lester. "There were fifty men working in here. First work I ever had was here — first work in the woods. Right after the war."

"What's that?" Lillian asked. She pointed across the clearing.

"That's Blackway's," said Lester.

Standing in a far corner of the barren ground was a house — in reality not a house, but an old bus, painted sky blue, without wheels, sitting down on its axles in the sawdust. Some of the windows were covered with plywood, and a stovepipe came out of one of them.

"It looks like a school bus," said Lillian.

"It is a school bus," said Lester. "They brought it in for a bunkhouse. That was after my time."

"They brought it here?" Lillian asked. "How? They didn't drive it. How did they get it in here?"

"Couldn't tell you," said Lester. "Boyd didn't do it. He was all done by then. Nobody's logged in here in twenty years. More than that. It's Blackway's now."

They left the trail and crossed the waste toward the bus. The sawdust was peculiar underfoot: soft and silent, but unmarked. They might have been walking on a bed. They might have been walking on the surface of the moon.

At the bus, Lester pushed open the doors and went up the steps past the driver's seat. Lillian followed him. Entering the bus, she paused. The rows of passengers' seats had been removed, and the rear two-thirds of the interior was taken up by three ranks of double-deck bunk beds hung on frames built of two-by-sixes. Forward of the bunks a wood-burning stove made from a fifty-five-gallon drum with the pipe let out one of the side windows. Between the stove and the driver's seat, in front, a small kitchen table and a single lawn chair, and on the table, an old railroad lantern painted red. The place was warm and close, smelling of sour ashes from the stove and, faintly, of kerosene.

Lester had come up ahead of Lillian. He was looking over the bunks. A sleeping bag lay on one of them; the others were nothing but bare plywood platforms without mattresses or blankets. An old double-bitted ax leaned in one corner. There was nothing else. Blackway was by himself in there.

"Don't much go in for housekeeping, does he?" said Lester.

"Is it really his place?" asked Lillian. "How do we know it is?"

"It's his," said Lester. "Or if it ain't, we'll find out soon enough."

"How?" asked Lillian. "We just sit in here and wait for him?"

"Not in here," said Lester. He turned to the door.

"Wait a minute —" Lillian began again. But Lester had left the bus and was outside looking over the ground before and behind it. The sun was nearly down on the mountain ridges to the west. It sank into a broad, tranquil bay of low cloud suffused with vermillion, scarlet, and rose. Long shadows advanced from the hillocks of sawdust, darted from the surrounding woods. The windows of the bus flashed and flared with the final light. The farthest hills, blue, turned purple, then gray, then black.

"We'll need a fire," said Lester. He dug in his pocket and came out with a book of matches, which he handed to Nate. "Make a good one," Lester told him. "Keep it going."

Before the door of the bus was a fire ring of blackened stones. A small pile of wood stood beside it, with a camp grill on legs, and a camp teapot nearby.

"What's the sense of that?" Lillian asked him. "He'll see it. He'll know somebody's here."

"That's right," said Lester. To Nate he said, "You best get more wood."

"Wait, Lester." Lillian stopped him. "Just wait a minute, okay? We can't do this. This isn't going to work."

Lester turned to her. "No?" he said.

"No," said Lillian. "It won't work. We need to get out of here."

"Can't," said Lester.

"What do you mean, can't?" Lillian demanded. "Why can't we? Nobody's here. We turn around and leave."

"No," said Lester. "We told you back there: We're down onto it. We've passed over. Now we got to go through."

"Why?" Lillian asked. "Because we took Blackway's keys? So what? We'll put them back. He won't know."

Lester looked at her.

"How will he know?" Lillian asked. "Are you saying he knows already? Are you saying he's coming now?"

"Go ahead," Lester said to Nate. "Get the wood." Lester had leaned his parcel against the bus when they went inside. Now he picked it up and turned to go.

"Wait," said Lillian. "Wait. Where are you going?"

"Don't know for sure," said Lester. "Not far."

Nate started walking toward the trees to find more wood.

"This is another trick, isn't it?" Lillian asked Lester.

"This ain't another trick," Lester told her. "This is the last trick. After this, I'm all out of tricks. This one's it. You better hope it works."

He left her.

Someone had taken one of the old passengers' seats from the bus and placed it before the fire ring. Lillian sat and waited for Nate to come back with the wood. Lester had disappeared around one of the sawdust hills. It was growing darker. Lillian was alone. She looked around her, above, behind. She got up and went to the corner of the bus. She peeped around the corner. Then she returned to the seat. The shadows spread, joined, the daylight departed. A single big star hung in the darkening sky over the black mountain rim. Lillian sat. She hugged herself and rocked back and forth a little. She waited for Nate.

Blackway was coming. Was he there already, in the woods, watching her right now? No. But he was close. Lillian could feel him nearby, she could feel him as a current of cold wet air off a brook or pool. Blackway was coming, and Nate and Lester couldn't, they wouldn't, get out of his way. They had to go through. Blackway held her little cat in his hands and left her on the step like a bloody rag. He was coming, and when he'd gone over Nate and Lester and nobody was left but Lillian, what would he do then?

Lillian held herself more tightly and looked into the fire.

Nate returned dragging a little dead fir tree, the whole thing. He dropped it beside the fire ring. Then he went into the bus and came out with the ax. He began hewing branches off the fir. With Lester's matches, he soon had a fire. As it caught and grew, the light failed entirely, and the night closed around them like a great dark hand.

"What's going to happen when he comes?" Lillian asked.

Nate stood before the fire and stared into the flames. His eyes didn't move, didn't blink. He didn't answer.

"Nate?" Lillian asked.

"Yo?"

"What happens when he comes?"

"Les?"

"Blackway."

Nate continued to gaze into the fire. He shrugged.

"I ain't afraid of Blackway," he said.

Lillian shook her head. "You keep on saying that," she said. "Sit down here, why don't you?"

"I'll stand," Nate said. He raised his eyes from the fire and looked at Lillian. He grinned.

"I ain't afraid of Blackway," said Nate. "But since Les ain't here, I'll tell you I won't be sorry when this is over."

"Come on," said Lillian. "Sit." She patted the seat beside her.

"I don't mind," said Nate.

"Poker game," said Whizzer. "Five, six of us used to get together: D.B., myself, Wingate, whoever else was around."

"Wingate was a regular, though," said D.B. "In fact, we mostly played at his place."

"Here, too," said Whizzer.

"But mainly at Wingate's," said D.B. "He rented a room at the old hotel in those days."

"Where was that?" Conrad asked.

"Right there on the edge of town," D.B. said. "Place that's the candle shop now. Wingate had a room in the back. We went there to play more than here."

"Wingate had a better table," said Whizzer. "And then, the hotel had a bar, so while you were playing you could order up a bunch of cold beers or a bottle of something to keep you sharp. It was more comfortable. Not everybody enjoys sitting around in here all day and all night."

"Don't they?" asked Coop. "Who doesn't?"

"Anyway," said D.B. "We'd play poker at Wingate's. And one night there was this guy who used to sit in who thought he was something of a card shark."

"Lucky Jim," said Whizzer.

"Thought he was pretty cute," said D.B. "And he was, sort of. He knew the games. He knew the odds. He usually came out ahead. We called him Lucky Jim."

"Lucky Jim?" asked Conrad.

"His real name was Hubert," said Whizzer. "Some kind of an engineer. He worked on the power dam. Worked for the Corps of Engineers."

"He's moved on," said D.B. "Lucky Jim has. Nobody was too unhappy when he did. Some thought he used to help out his side a little. He had very fast hands."

"He didn't mind if you thought that, either," said Whizzer.

"No, he didn't," said D.B. "That was part of his game, the idea that maybe he was helping himself a little in the deal but you weren't sure. It was kind of like a little bluff he ran."

"So one night we're at Wingate's, and Lucky Jim deals out a hand of short stud," said Whizzer.

"Five-card," said D.B. "There was Jim, Wingate, Whizzer, and me."

"Lucky Jim's dealing," said Whizzer. "Short stud game. He deals out four hands. And high man is himself with — what was it?"

"Jack of Diamonds," said D.B.

Lester walked around the nearest of the sawdust hills and began to climb up to its top. On the soft ground he went silently. He wasn't going far, but he didn't want the other two to know that. He didn't want them to know where he was. When Blackway showed up, surprise would be what Lester had. It would be about all he had, and surprise means nobody's to know. Not your side, not the other side, nobody.

From the top of the little hill he looked down at one end of the bus, fifty feet away. He could just see Lillian sitting before the fire ring. Nate had gone for wood. He was out of sight. This spot was no good. You couldn't see the ground in front of the bus. You couldn't see, and the bus was too far away. Lester now saw he would need to be no farther than a few yards from the fire ring when Blackway came. Closer would be better. That meant inside the bus — or, better, it meant up on the roof. The roof was the best place for what he had to do. Blackway, when he came, might know he was into something more here than a couple of kids. He would know it. He would be looking around for trouble. But Lester would be right on top of him, and Blackway wouldn't be looking up.

Lester didn't think he could climb onto the top of the bus without Nate and Lillian's knowing he was up there. He'd have to wait till Blackway appeared, till he and Nate had gotten into it. That way, maybe none of them would hear him. Meantime he'd have to get closer to the bus, around the other side. For that he'd have to wait for full dark. He watched Nate drag the tree out of the woods and start trimming the branches with the ax. Lester had a little time. He waited.

He tried to recall the big yard at Boyd's. Was this it? It might have been. You couldn't tell. It was different then. No sawdust. Boyd hadn't had a mill. The logs they'd cut over the winter they'd driven out down the river in the spring. So, no sawdust desert. And no bus. Boyd had had a log bunkhouse. Boyd also had stables, a kitchen, a shop, but if anything was left of any of them today, and if this was where they had stood, then the sawdust covered them.

Directly across the open ground from Lester's position, a big pine tree rose thirty feet above the tops of the younger growth surrounding it. There had been a big one behind the bunkhouse at Boyd's. Was that the same tree? Lester couldn't tell from here. Up close, he might know it. The men had left that tree standing for a purpose — if you believed them. It wasn't just another pine, they told the young Lester. It was a woods wife. A what? There was a knothole in the trunk, they'd told him, at just the right height for — well, try it yourself, kid. Fifty men stuck out there in the woods all winter. Not old men, either. Nothing to do but work and eat and sleep. No women. How much checkers can you play? You got to feel like you couldn't stand it any longer. Then, they told Lester, what you did, you gave some business to your woods wife. You got a handful of lard from the kitchen, you got that knothole greased up pretty good, and you went right at it. Woods wives, they called those convenient trees, or pussy pines. If you believed them.

Lester didn't believe them. Though it was true some of those old boys, some of those old-time choppers, were different. You could say they were colorful. You could say they were individuals. The point was, if they didn't carry on with the trees, it wasn't because they thought doing so was in poor taste.

They took a good look at Lester, too, didn't they, when he joined the crew at Boyd's: only a kid, small, curly-headed, and cute as a cricket? Yes, they had looked him over pretty close. First night, Boyd himself had come into the bunkhouse carrying a big butcher's knife he'd brought from the kitchen. He'd made sure they all saw him give the knife to Lester, he'd made sure they heard him tell the boy to keep it by him in his bunk and to go ahead and use it if he had to.

Boyd himself was no common piece of work: a three-hundred-pound Irishman with a face like a great ham. He was probably the same way as the worst of the choppers, but he made a joke of it. Boyd had been a bosun's mate in the Pacific during the war and he upheld the great tradition of the World War Two United States Navy: If it moves, fuck it; if it doesn't move, paint it. Though it's true that in the woods there wasn't much to paint.

"You see this, me boy?" said Boyd, handing the butcher's knife to Lester. "See this? Any of these animals interferes with you so you don't like it, you cut it right off him, see? Lop it right off. That'll slow him down."

"What if he does like it?" one of the choppers asked Boyd.

"Then he can give me back me fucking knife," said Boyd.

Years ago. Years and years. From the top of his hill Lester watched the fire Nate had built. He watched Nate and Lillian sitting together before the fire, talking. He saw the firelight shine on Lillian's hair, where it lay down her back. He thought of Lillian's hair spread out behind her, fanned out, on a grassy bank, on a pillow, Lillian lying back on her hair. You can keep your pussy pines. But, no. Not likely. Not for him. Too many years. Too many years and too few moments. What was he? An old man with a dirty mind. He wouldn't know what to do with her, would most likely turn and run. Not like some. Not like Blackway. Lester thought of Lillian letting down her hair, fanning it out, spreading it for Blackway. That wouldn't be happening, either, would it? Blackway might have picked on the wrong girl this time, it looked like.

The firelight made the night black. He could move anytime now. Still he sat, waited. Presently he unwrapped the parcel he'd been carrying. Inside was his uncle Walt's old goose gun. It was practically an antique: a ten-gauge, with double barrels as big as water pipes, the kind of gun meant to be mounted in the bow of a skiff. The next gun bigger about got you into the field artillery, as Walt used to say. Walt and his wife had had girls, no boys, and when Walt died his wife had given the gun to Lester. He'd hung on to it, less from having any use for such a thing than from not liking to get rid of it. It stood in a corner at Lester's. Irene hated it, she wouldn't dust it, wouldn't touch it. Then lately, when everybody got so worried about the terrorists and the Islamers and them, Lester had gone out and got a box of shells for Walt's gun. Irene had mocked him, and Lester didn't say she was wrong, but the way he reasoned it, he had the gun anyway. It fired. And nobody knew what was going to happen, did they? Did all those people, a couple of thousand people, when they went to work that morning in their office buildings, know that before lunch they were all going to be burned up and their buildings down in the street? They didn't. What Lester did know, what he knew for sure, was that any Islamer or anybody else who got in front of Walt's goose gun was going to be out of the fight for good.

Lester stood, a little painfully. He broke open the gun and took two shells from his pants pocket: fat red buckshot shells with shiny brass bases. They looked like things you might hang on your Christmas tree. Lester loaded both barrels. About time to do it, now, about time to get to work. Lester shut and locked the gun, then started quietly back down the hill in the dark.

"Jack of Diamonds to Lucky Jim," said Whizzer. "Not much else on the table. We bet. Everybody's in. Jim deals the third card."

"Still nothing much," said D.B. "Until Jim gives himself another Jack."

"Wingate's showing two Clubs," said Whizzer. "What did you have?"

"Nothing," said D.B. "We bet. Lucky Jim deals the fourth. Wingate pulls a third Club."

"Jim pulls — what?" said Whizzer. "Did he get his other Jack then?"

"No," said D.B. "He got a red trey. Jim's got a pair of Jacks, only color on the table. He bets ten bucks. I quit. Jim, Whiz, and Wingate have the game. Pot's right. Jim deals the last card."

"Jack of Hearts to Lucky Jim," said Whizzer. "That's three Jacks showing."

"Another Club for Wingate," said D.B. "Four flush in Clubs looking at a possible four Jacks."

"Or a possible full boat," Whizzer said, "if Jim had paired a down trey. Either way he beats Wingate's flush."

"He does, if he's got it," said D.B.

"Not bad for a short game," said Whizzer. "Lucky Jim's high hand. He shoves in twenty bucks."

"For this table, that's a big bet," said D.B.

"Too big for me," said Whizzer. "I quit."

Nate and Lillian sat side by side on the seat before the fire.

"What's Lester going to do when Blackway comes?" Lillian asked Nate.

"Don't know," said Nate.

"I'm not wrong about the gun, am I?" Lillian asked. "That is a gun he's been carrying around, right?"

"Don't know," Nate said. "I guess it is."

"Blackway won't be scared off by a gun," said Lillian.

Lillian watched Nate lean forward and take hold of a little branch of the fir tree he had dragged to the fire ring. He broke it off and poked its end into the fire. The dry fir caught and blazed quickly up, sputtering and snapping.

"I ain't scared of Blackway," Nate said.

"Yes, you are," said Lillian. "You say you aren't, but you are. Everybody is. This thing isn't going to work. You can't do it. You and Lester together cannot do this."

"Maybe not," Nate said.

"Why, then? Why keep at it?"

Nate shook his head.

"We came here," he said. "We are here. We came this far. We got to go through. You got to go through. That's what Les says."

"Les, Les. Fuck Les," said Lillian.

"Take it easy, now," said Nate.

"Hello, sweetheart," said Blackway. "Who's this?"

"Wingate sees him," said D.B.

"And then," said Whizzer, "Wingate shoves in twenty more."

"So now it's right up to Lucky Jim, ain't it?" said D.B. "He knows what he's got. Maybe he's got his four Jacks. Maybe he's got his boat. Maybe he don't. Then what? Trip Jacks. Not too bad, but not good enough if Wingate's got his flush. Does he?"

"One way to find out," said Whizzer. "You got to go through."

"You got to go through," said D.B. "It's a learning experience."

"So Lucky Jim sees Wingate," said Whizzer. "And Wingate turns it over."

"Flush in Clubs," said D.B. "He's got it."

"Jim don't," said Whizzer. "Jim's got his three Jacks."

"Jim's got air," said D.B.

"Most of two hundred bucks on the table," said Whizzer. "Jim's pissed."

"He's pissed," said D.B. "Chucks in his cards, gets up from the table, and stomps off out of the room. And I said to Wingate, 'Well, that was a game.'"

"And Wingate says," Whizzer went on, "'I knew he didn't have it.' And I asked him —"

"And you asked him," D.B. interrupted, "'How did you know? It was his deal.'"

"What with Lucky Jim having fast hands, you see?" Whizzer said. "'How did you know?' I asked Wingate. 'It was his deal.' And Wingate said —"

"And Wingate said," D.B. picked up. But Whizzer cut him off:

"'His deal,' Wingate said. 'My deck.'"

Lillian drew herself back into the seat and looked at Blackway. She couldn't see his face. He stood in the shadow on the opposite side of the fire, just outside its light, about twenty feet from them. He had on a long, sweeping coat, a kind of duster. It fell almost to his heels, and in the play of firelight and shadow it made Blackway look even taller than he was, and he was tall enough.

"Who's your friend, sweetheart?" Blackway asked. He stepped closer to the fire and looked narrowly across it at Lillian and Nate.

"This is a baby you got here, sweetheart," Blackway said. "Another baby. Come on, where's the men?"

Lillian couldn't answer him. She opened her mouth to say something, but she couldn't. She couldn't speak. She looked at Nate, who had gotten to his feet. Blackway began taking off the duster.

Nate said nothing, but went right at Blackway, leaping over the fire to reach him. He got to Blackway before Blackway had shed his coat, but Blackway was ready for him. He threw the coat at Nate and stepped aside, letting Nate go past him and tripping him as he did. Nate pitched down headfirst and Blackway kicked him hard in the side as he lay, but Nate was up again in an instant and back at Blackway. Blackway let him come. He feinted right and swung at Nate with his left fist, but Nate got around it and hit Blackway on the side of the head. Lillian could hear that hit, a sound like the bursting of a paper sack.

Blackway staggered two steps to his right and nearly fell. He put one hand on the ground to brace himself and sprang back at Nate, who stood bent a little at the hip to favor his side, as though Blackway's kick had hurt him. Blackway came at him low and tried to butt him in the midsection, but Nate caught Blackway's head under his arm and clamped it there, then hit his jaw, twice, three times, with short downward blows as though struck with a hammer. Blackway went down beside the fire. He shook his head and spat out blood. Nate shouldn't have let him recover, not even for a second, but Nate was hurt, too. Blackway was on all fours near the little fir tree lying ready to be burned, near the ax Nate had used to chop it up.

"Look out!" Lillian whispered.

Nate didn't hear her. He threw himself at Blackway. Blackway grasped the ax and rolled out of the way of Nate, kicking up at him. His boot got Nate under the right kneecap. Neither man had made a sound before then, but with the kick to his knee Nate let out a yell and collapsed to one side. He grabbed his knee in both hands and rolled on the ground.

Lillian watched Blackway stand and go to Nate, the ax in his right hand. He kicked Nate again, this time in the side of the head. Nate went out. Blackway stood over him. He straddled Nate as Nate lay beside the fire. Blackway looked across the fire at Lillian. Lillian looked back at him. She saw that Blackway's face, lit by the fire, was badly broken and cut on one side where Nate had beaten him, but she saw more than that. She saw Blackway was old. "You're old," she whispered. "You're finished." Blackway was going the way of all the others. He was old, and he was hurt. He was in trouble here, and he knew it. But he wasn't done yet. He stood over Nate and looked across the red, flaring firelight at Lillian. He raised the heavy double-bitted ax high above his head, as though he were about to split a chunk.

"Watch this, sweetheart," said Blackway.

Lillian tried to cry out No, or Stop, or Don't, or anything at all. She had drawn in her breath to say it when the entire sky exploded above and behind her in a bright flash and a blast and a sudden, passing impact, like a high wind, that snatched at her hair and blew the fire aside and seemed to pluck Blackway from where he stood above Nate's body and fling him backward into the darkness beyond the firelight.

Lillian might have lost consciousness for a moment. Her ears rang and her eyes were dazzled by the flash. She was aware of sitting up on the seat and looking across the fire at Lester. Lester was there now. He stood beside Nate, who had come to and sat up. Nate was rubbing his knee. Both of them were looking at Blackway, whose boots, unmoving, Lillian could see extending from the dark into the firelight. Lester held propped on his right shoulder a long, heavy gun, its barrels pointing up into the sky. He and Nate were looking down at Blackway.

"Jeesum," said Lester.

16

CONSPIRACIES

Whizzer drained his beer. Conrad pulled three more out of the case beside him and handed them to Whizzer, Coop, and D.B. He took the last for himself.

"So," Conrad said, "Wingate had stacked the deck, right? He had a stacked deck. He switched it in. That's what you're saying?"

"I never thought so," said D.B. "It was a straight game. Wingate won it."

"If you believe that," Whizzer said, "you'll believe anything."

"Why?" D.B. asked him.

"He said it, didn't he? You heard him. Wingate. He said, 'His deal. My deck.'"

"Oh, well," said Coop. "That's just Wingate, ain't it?"

"What do you mean?" D.B. asked him.

"Just him talking," said Coop.

"Wingate don't just talk," said Whizzer.

"Don't he?" Coop asked.

"We been over this," said D.B.

"We have," said Whizzer. "Wingate cooked the deck because he wanted to show that guy Jim what's what, and because he wanted Jim out of the game. Worked, too."

"I still say it was an honest game," said D.B.

Whizzer laughed at him.

"Suspicious old boy, ain't he?" Coop asked Conrad.

"Me?" asked Whizzer.

"You," said Coop. "Wingate stacked the deck on that guy. The troopers had the dope business fixed with Blackway, back there. Blackway had a secret weapon he used to bust up Scotty and them at the Fort, that time. Somebody came into the Towns on skis that winter and took those Frenchmen. I bet it was the Russians, that time. Everything's a plot, ain't it? Whiz probably reckons it was the Young Republicans killed JFK, it was the Young Democrats got together and flew into those buildings in New York."

"Conspiracies," said Conrad.

"There you go," said Coop. "Whiz reckons everything's a conspiracy."

"All I do," said Whizzer, "is look around. Think things over. Use common sense. Try it yourself. See where it gets you. Somebody is pulling the strings. It ain't me. It ain't you. Am I wrong about that?"

"You're not wrong about us," said Conrad. "You're wrong because there are no strings."

"There you go," said Coop.

"You boys," said Whizzer, "have got a lot to learn. I'm glad it ain't any of you's got to go up against Blackway today."

"Speaking of which," said D.B. "I wonder if they've caught up with him yet. They might have."

"No," said Whizzer. "They won't do it till it's dark. They'll wait for tonight."

"Not Nate the Great," said Coop. "He won't wait. He don't know how."

"No, but Les does," said Whizzer.

"Right," said D.B. "By himself, that kid just goes in, he just goes for it. Blackway eats him up. Not Les. Les will wait. He'll wait till it's right. He knows the tricks. With Les behind him, Nate has a shot."

"Not by himself, he don't," said Coop. "Put Les into it with him? Then, maybe."

"You could call that a conspiracy, I guess," said Whizzer. "Couldn't you?"

Coop laughed. "Okay, Whiz," he said.

For a moment the men drank their beer in silence. The late-afternoon sun was in the window of the office. It lay in a square on the floor, it lit the dust on the window glass, it lit the dust in the air.

"And then, when it's over, what?" Conrad asked at last.

"What, for who?" Whizzer asked him. "For Blackway?"

"For Nate and Lester," said Conrad.

"Oh," said Whizzer. "Back to loading blocks, it looks like. What else?"

"What have you got them building out there, anyway?" Conrad asked.

"Nothing," said Whizzer.

"What are they stacking the blocks for, then?"

"Nothing," said Whizzer.

"Keeping busy," said D.B.

"Giving them something to do," said Coop.

"I see," said Conrad.

"I don't," said Coop. "Well, with Les I do. Les is old. He's about got done. But Nate the Great ain't. He's a kid. You put him to work around here, doing one thing and another — and that's all right, I guess. Far as it goes. But what about when you're gone? When this place is gone? What does he do then, Nate the Great?"

"Gets a real job," said D.B.

"How?" asked Coop. "Doing what? He don't know nothing. He ain't been no place but here or done nothing but what you gave him to do. What's it going to be for him?"

"He'll be fine," said Whizzer. "He's a good kid. There's more to Nate the Great than you know."

"Maybe there is," said Coop. "But I don't see where he fits anymore, is what I'm saying. You know what it is today: You're either a brain surgeon or you're drawing welfare."

"Is that right?" Whizzer asked him. "Which of them is you?"

"Neither," said Coop. "I don't mean for me, for us. We had our day. We managed all right. I mean for Nate, for the kids. There ain't a lot of room for them anymore, it looks like."

"It's a conspiracy," said Conrad.

"It is," said D.B.

"*Another* conspiracy," said Coop.

"It damned well is," said D.B. "But not everything is. That game at Wingate's, that was a straight game."

"If you believe that," said Whizzer, "we'll tell you another one."

"Go ahead," said D.B. "Tell me."

"Not today," said Whizzer. He looked over at the case of beer beside Conrad. "It's by you, ain't it?" he asked Conrad.

"Not anymore," Conrad said.

"All gone?" Whizzer asked him.

"We had it," said Conrad.

"We did?" Coop asked. "That was a light case, then, wasn't it?"

"Well," said D.B., "you got to take into account the source."

"Scotty?" asked Conrad.

"Scotty kind of runs the light-case department," said Coop.

"Kind of a specialty of his," said D.B.

"Like bar fighting," said Coop.

Whizzer finished his beer, set the empty down on the floor beside his cart. The sun had left the window, and the room had grown dark, but none of the four of them moved to turn on a light.

"You know," Whizzer said, "you don't have to worry about Nate the Great. He'll be fine. He can make it on his own. Sure, he can. And if he can't, well, I expect I'll be around for a while yet."

"Good to know," said D.B.

Whizzer looked at the clock on the wall of the office.

"Fact is," he said, "it's probably for the best Scotty brought in a light case. We can't sit in here drinking all afternoon."

"We already did," said Coop.

17

GO WITH ME

Lester drove. He drove the three of them in Blackway's truck down to where they had left the other vehicle. They bounced along the rough track they had come over on foot hours earlier. Lillian rode between the two men. She looked from one to the other of them, trying to make them out in the shadows. She swayed against them in the dark.

Before, at the camp, following Lester's shot, they had held Lillian back. They hadn't let her see. When she started toward where Blackway lay beyond the firelight, Nate had stopped her.

"Stay where you are," Lester said. "You don't want to look at this."

From the roof of the bus, Lester had given Blackway both barrels of Uncle Walt's goose gun. That close, the blast had struck Blackway as a dense column of buckshot about a foot long. Lester was no sharpshooter, he'd hardly fired the gun before, and he'd been aiming down. Therefore he'd been a little high. The load had hit Blackway at the collarbone. It had taken his head right off his shoulders. The ruined head lay in the shadows at a distance from the rest of Blackway. It had rolled about a yard.

"You want to get that?" Lester asked Nate.

"You get it," Nate said.

Lillian sat before the fire, keeping it burning while Lester and Nate went to work. They dragged Blackway out of the clearing and into the woods. She could hear them thrashing in the woods. In fifteen minutes they returned, smothered the fire, and got ready to start walking out.

"We're leaving him here?" Lillian asked.

"It looks like we would, don't it?" Lester said. "He's heavy. You want to tote him back to town, you go ahead."

"What if somebody comes looking for him?"

"Who?"

"What if somebody finds him, though?"

"They won't," said Lester. "He won't last long. Not up here, he won't. Coyotes, foxes, buzzards, crows, all them. They'll find him. They've found him already. They'll break him up. In a week there won't be nothing left of Blackway."

"That was part of it, wasn't it?" Lillian asked him. "That was part of it, too. Your plan?"

"Sure," said Lester. "What did you think? Did you think we were going to lay him out in the parlor in his best suit?"

"No," said Lillian. "But I didn't think — I mean, I thought the gun was to scare him off. Not kill him."

"You knew better," said Lester. "You can't scare Blackway off. You knew that. You said it yourself. Blackway don't scare. He don't bluff. We told you: If you start with Blackway, you got to be ready to go all the way through."

"You're talking about him like he was still alive," said Lillian.

"Well, he ain't," said Lester. "You wish he was?"

"I didn't say that," said Lillian.

The truck bounced and bounded over the track, and its headlights flew up into the treetops, then plunged down to the ground in front of them. Now and then a deer or some other animal, pale in their lights, disappeared into the woods ahead.

"Blackway was a bad guy," said Lester. "He was big around here because there wasn't nothing he wouldn't do and he made sure everybody knew it. He got one thing wrong, though. He thought he was the only guy like that. That's why he walked into our business here tonight. I was pretty sure he would: Blackway never thought nobody would go as far as him. Sometimes, if the worst guy around makes that same mistake, the second worst guy has a chance."

"The second worst guy, that's you?" Lillian asked him.

"Not anymore," said Lester.

When they reached the turnout where they had left Nate's truck, they stopped. Lester drove on alone in Blackway's truck, with Nate and Lillian following him in Nate's, Lillian driving.

"Where are we going?" Lillian asked Nate.

"Leave the truck off, it looks like," said Nate.

"Where?" Lillian asked.

"Wherever Les thinks," said Nate.

Nate was hurt in his side, where he had taken Blackway's boot. He leaned against the door of the truck. He held his side.

"I want to look at that," said Lillian.

"It ain't nothing," said Nate. He nodded ahead. "There he goes."

Lester was turning off the highway. Lillian followed him. They had come back to the High Line. The long white building lay before them, a pallid hulk. The parking lot was empty. No window showed a light. The place might have been deserted.

Lester stopped Blackway's truck in front of the High Line, shut off the engine, and joined Nate and Lillian. Lillian moved over beside Nate, and Lester got behind the wheel.

"Okay," he said. "Let's go."

"We're leaving it here?" Lillian asked.

"Sure," said Lester. "We got to leave it somewhere. Let Stu and them figure it out."

At that moment they heard the laughter of the crazy woman coming from one of the rooms.

"*Hee-hee-heee-heeee-eeee.*"

"I'd think they'd shut her up," said Lester. "They did before."

"They can't hear her," said Lillian. "Nobody hears her. She's all alone."

"I guess she is, at that," said Lester.

They drove out of the High Line lot and got back on the highway, pointed toward home. In the truck Lillian turned to Nate. She wanted to see his side. She switched on the overhead light.

"Take off your shirt," Lillian told Nate.

"What?"

"Take off your shirt. I want to see where you're hurt. Come on."

"It ain't that bad."

"Come on," said Lillian. She helped Nate out of his T-shirt and looked at his side. Nate's midsection on the left was badly bruised all up and down. Lillian laid her hand on the injured place.

"Does that hurt you?" she asked Nate.

"It ain't that bad," said Nate.

Lillian pressed him gently with her hand.

"Ow," said Nate.

"Leave the boy alone," said Lester.

"He's hurt," said Lillian.

"He's fine," said Lester. "He'll be fine. What he needs is for Nurse Rowena to take a look at it. Nurse Rowena will know just what to do, I expect."

Lillian touched Nate's bruised side lightly with her fingertips.

"Does that hurt?" she asked again.

"No," said Nate.

Lillian moved her hand over his side.

"Should I go on?" Lillian asked him.

"I don't mind," said Nate.

"That'll do," said Lester. "Put your clothes back on. Look at the two of you. Carrying on. I don't know about you people."

They drew up in front of Lester's place. He got out of the truck and shut the door. He looked up at the sky. Above the sleeping settlement the heaven was full of stars, slowly wheeling, but the night was as yet perfectly still. In Lester's front yard, the whirligigs were unmoving: The duck didn't fly, the chopper didn't chop, the Indian didn't paddle his canoe.

Lillian moved over behind the wheel. Lester stood beside the truck.

"Well," he said.

"You did it," said Lillian.

"'Course we did," said Lester. "What did you think?"

"I don't know," said Lillian. "I thought you couldn't, then I thought maybe you could, then I thought you couldn't. I knew you couldn't. Blackway —"

"Forget about Blackway," said Lester. "Blackway's all done. We said we'd take care of him for you. Well, we have. I'd shut up about Blackway from now on, if I was you."

Lester got the goose gun out of the back of the truck and returned to the window. He peered into the truck. Nate had gone to sleep.

"You'd better get him on home," he said.

"He ought to see a doctor," said Lillian. "I'm afraid he's got cracked ribs."

"He ain't got nothing," said Lester. "He's fine. You can't hurt him."

Lillian smiled in the dark. "Okay," she said.

"Go on," said Lester. He stepped back from the truck and waited for her to pull away.

"Lester?"

"Go on, now," said Lester.

Lillian nodded. She put the truck in gear and drove away. Lester turned, rested the goose gun on his shoulder, and walked slowly to his door. At the door he looked down the road where Lillian's rear lights went around the bend and disappeared. Where were those two going? Not to the ball game. Not to the picnic. Not to church. To someplace where he couldn't follow them. Not even the first worst man could follow them where they were going. Not if he was old. Lester had got bad too late, it looked like. He saw again Lillian's hair, loose, tangled, falling down her back, down her shoulders. Good luck to her, he thought. Good luck to them both. They'll need it, everybody does. For him, what he'd had to do he'd done, and for the rest, well, maybe next time. Next time?

Lester let himself into his house. As he shut the door behind him, one of the whirligigs in the yard began lazily to turn over, then another, set in motion by the first faint arrival of the little breeze that comes before the dawn on summer mornings.

"Nate?"

"Yo."

"Are you asleep?"

"No."

"How's your side?"

"Not too bad. I'll be fine, the way Les says."

"Right. Your girlfriend. What's her name? Rowena? Rowena will take care of it, won't she? She'll kiss it and make it well. Won't she?"

"She ain't my girlfriend."

"What is she, then?"

"I don't know. Well, she might be my cousin, I guess. Let's see: Her stepdad is my mother's cousin. I think. Does that make her and me cousins?"

"I don't know."

"If it does, we're cousins. Rowena works at the clinic. One day this spring she was on her way to work and her car conked out. I came along, gave her a ride to the clinic. Les was at the clinic when we drove up. Seven AM. Ever since, Les has got it fixed we're going together. Me and Rowena. We ain't."

"Don't you have one, then?"

"One what?"

"A girlfriend?"

"No."

"Why not?"

"No need."

"No need?"

They had stopped in front of the house where Lillian had been living with Kevin Bay, then without him, a house in the woods. She turned off the engine and the headlights, and they sat together in the dark. Not in the dark, but in the beginning of the beginning of the first paleness, the imperceptible lightening, the gray whisper of the dawn.

"No need? I don't believe you. You don't need anybody?"

"Why would I?"

"To be with you. To go with you."

"Go where?"

"Anywhere. Wherever you go."

"You need that, not me."

"Then why did you go with me today?"

"Yesterday."

"Why did you go with me yesterday?"

"Because you asked me to."

"No, I didn't. I didn't ask you. I didn't want you. I wanted that other one, the one who wasn't there."

"Scotty."

"I wanted him. Not you. I said so. You heard what I said. You didn't have to go with me. Why did you?"

"Boss said I was to."

"You mean Whizzer?"

"Him and Les."

"You do what they tell you?"

"Sure."

"Why?"

"No reason not to."

"No reason except it almost got you killed. No reason except the person you were trying to help was laughing at you. Me. I was laughing at you. I thought you were — well, you know what I thought. You went with me anyway. No dummy who's just following orders does that. Does he?"

Nate shrugged. He didn't reply. They sat in the truck and watched the day resolve itself before them in a shifting silver screen of fog, light, shadow, and mass.

"Does he?"

"Who?"

"You. No dumb kid would have done what you did, would have gone with me the way I was, the way you did. A dumb kid doesn't do that, does he?"

"How about if I asked you a question?"

"What question?"

"Before, when he was after you — that one we left back up there. Why didn't you run, like they asked you? Why didn't you just get away?"

"I was different."

"Was?"

"I thought I was. I wanted to be. The boy I was with, before?"

"Kevin?"

"Kevin was different. He was smart. He could talk. Schmuckville, he called this place. East Schmuckville. It wasn't for him. Not for Kevin. He was going to get out. He was going to do things. Like me."

"Sure."

"And then, Blackway? Blackway went past Kevin like a big truck on the highway when you're riding a bicycle. Blackway just blew him away. Poor Kevin."

"Poor Kevin."

"For a day, two days, he didn't leave the house. All he wanted to do was smoke dope and watch TV. Then he ran. He ran and he left me."

"Well, that's Kevin, ain't it?"

"Is it? Did you know Kevin?"

"Sure. He was a year ahead of me. Come to that, we're cousins, Kevin and me."

"You are? Kevin's your cousin. Rowena's your cousin. Is everybody in town your cousin?"

"Pretty much."

"When he ran, Kevin, I decided I wasn't going to. I picked up a little knife, a paring knife, and I left the house, alone. If Blackway was out there, I was going to take him on. I was going to take Blackway on with a paring knife."

"What's a paring knife?"

"Oh, like for in the kitchen. A little kitchen knife. But, do you see, about Kevin? Kevin ran. He was different, but he ran."

"Can't blame him, can you? I guess he didn't have a what's-it knife. 'Course he ran."

"You didn't run."

"I ain't Kevin."

"No, you aren't."

"I ain't different."

"No."

"That's enough about me and Kevin, now, ain't it?"

"It is."

In the woods the first birds had begun to call, tentatively, in simple, hesitant notes — *plink, plonk* — like the hammering of sleepy smiths up in the trees.

"Nate?"

"Yo."

"What do you say? Will you go with me again?"

"When?"

"Now?"

"I don't mind."

"Whizzer didn't tell you to, you know."

"I know."

"Lester didn't tell you to."

"I know."

"I'm not them."

"No, you ain't."

Lillian opened the door of the truck and got out. She shut the door. She turned to Nate.

"Well?"

"I don't mind."

18

THE GROUND

Conrad sat down on the edge of the bed and bent to untie his shoes. Betsy was sitting on her side of the bed with her legs crossed, watching the national news report on the TV. There were fires in the West, in the dry mountains: Colorado, Arizona, places like that were burning.

"Those poor people," said Betsy.

"Do you know a girl named Lillian?" Conrad asked her. "Late twenties, beautiful long brown hair, used to work at the nursery?"

"At the nursery?" Betsy said. "No. I don't know her. I can't keep track of the girls in their late twenties with beautiful long brown hair who work at the nursery. There are too many of them. None of them stays more than a week. Edie Lippincott can't keep them."

"What's the matter with her?" asked Conrad.

"Edie? Edie's a dragon," said Betsy.

Conrad watched the TV for a minute. What was needed out there was rain. But there was no rain.

"This girl was at the mill today," he said.

"She was? I'll bet Lonnie liked that."

"You're right," said Conrad. "He did. They all did."

"The old goat. Were you really there all day?"

"Yes."

"God," said Betsy. "I'd think you'd bore yourself to death."

"Why?" said Conrad. "It's not boring. Not at all. You ought to stop down there yourself sometime."

"No, thank you," said Betsy.

"Whizzer's a gallant old boy, in his own way," said Conrad. "He's got a lot going against him and not much for. And he is your brother."

"He is," said Betsy. "He might as well not be. Lonnie never paid much attention to me. Why would he? I was eleven years younger, and plus, of course, I was a girl. Lonnie and them don't have much use for girls."

"That's not what you just said."

"That's exactly what I just said."

They watched the TV together for a couple of minutes. Three children were missing in Florida, three little girls. They'd been gone for four days. Nobody believed those children were still alive, but thousands were looking for them. All over Florida, Alabama, Georgia, they were searching. Friends and family members of the missing girls were talking to the TV reporters. The girls' parents were in seclusion.

"Those poor people," said Betsy.

Conrad stood up to take off his shirt and pants.

"What did she want, the girl from the nursery?" Betsy asked him.

"She was in trouble with some guy she'd done something to," said Conrad. "He was threatening her, following her. She went to the sheriff. He couldn't do anything. The guy hadn't acted, you see. The sheriff told her to go to Whizzer's for help. Whizzer sent her off with one of the kids who hangs around the mill and an older guy named Lester."

"Lester Speed?" Betsy asked.

"I guess so."

"I didn't think Lester Speed was still alive," said Betsy.

"They went off looking for the guy who'd been after the girl," said Conrad. "He sounded like a fairly serious kind of a guy. They were going up into the mountains to find him. He lives up there."

"Blackway," said Betsy.

"You know him, too?" asked Conrad.

"By reputation," said Betsy. "He's been around for years."

"Who is he?"

"He's like the village criminal," said Betsy. "He's what we've got up here instead of organized crime."

"From what they were saying this afternoon," said Conrad, "you might have some of that, too."

"I wouldn't doubt it," said Betsy. "It's called progress."

Now the TV was reporting a story from out on the Plains. At a wildlife park in Nebraska, a buffalo had gone off its rocker and charged into a group of tourists, killing two and injuring a dozen. A state policeman had shot the buffalo. But the TV reporter was alarmed, as there are buffalo by the hundreds of thousands all over Nebraska, Wyoming, and both Dakotas.

"Those poor people," said Betsy.

"Those poor buffalo," said Conrad.

"You had enough of this?" Betsy asked him.

"More than," said Conrad.

Betsy turned off the TV, slipped under the sheet, and lay on her back. Conrad got in beside her. He turned off the light. After a moment Betsy spoke again.

"Don't worry about Lonnie," she told Conrad. "He's not neglected."

"No, he's not," said Conrad. "He's got the others."

"Them," said Betsy, "and, plus, he comes here Thanksgiving, Christmas, so on. Doesn't he? And by and by, when he really gets past taking care of himself, I expect he'll move in here, live here. With us. He'll have to."

"I expect he will," said Conrad.

"You'll love that. Won't you?"

"I expect I will."

"Do you want to go to sleep now?"

"I don't mind."

Betsy patted his stomach under the sheet.

"You're really going native on me, aren't you, boy?" she asked.

"You know?" Conrad said. "I'm down there sitting around with them, listening, and of course I don't know the ground."

"Mmmm," said Betsy.

"I don't know what they're talking about, half the time, or who," Conrad went on. "But I have this feeling. The more I hear, the more I have it."

"Mmmm?" said Betsy.

"This feeling that Whizzer and the rest of them are all sitting inside a spaceship," Conrad said. "A rocket ship. They're in there, and the ship is traveling. It's moving. It's going so fast. It's going at light speed, you know? And so, the men who are on it don't get old, do they? That's what Einstein said. Isn't it? They don't change. Time doesn't pass for them. Time stretches. It stretches, or it shrinks. Or something. They're out of time. You know?"

"No, Einstein," said Betsy. "I don't know. I don't have any idea what you're talking about, and I don't think you do, either."

"That's possible, too," said Conrad.

19

MORE EARLY RISERS

Coming from the head in his cart, Whizzer rolled past the wide mill door. He looked out, stopped, backed up, looked again. Across the yard, behind the morning fog, a truck. The sheriff's truck. Whizzer got his cart turned and rolled out the door into the yard. Wingate left his truck and went to meet him.

"Morning," said Whizzer.

"You're up early," said Wingate.

"Can't seem to sleep much anymore," said Whizzer.

"No," said Wingate. He waited, watching Whizzer in his cart.

Whizzer looked around the yard where the mist hung in curtains of silver and gold as the sun rose above it.

"Going to burn off all right," said Whizzer. "Going to be another good one."

"Very likely."

Whizzer could hear in the woods around the yard the sudden soft patter of drops falling as the mist condensed on the trees and showered briefly down.

"'Course," said Whizzer, "it might come on to rain."

"It might."

"Yes," said Whizzer, "it might, at that. Can I buy you a cup of coffee, inside? It's just made."

"Was that girl here yesterday, that girl Blackway's been after?" asked Wingate.

"You mean that girl Blackway's been after?" Whizzer asked.

"That one."

"You mean that girl with the long hair?"

"Was she here yesterday?"

"She was," said Whizzer. "Told us you'd sent her."

Wingate didn't reply.

"Told us she'd gone to you because she's scared of Blackway," Whizzer said. "You said she was to come here and find Scotty."

"That's right."

"Scotty wasn't here."

"I saw Scotty," Wingate said. "Last night. He said they had some kind of trouble at the Fort yesterday."

"Trouble?" Whizzer asked.

"Some kind of fight."

"Trouble at the Fort?" Whizzer said. "Well, sure. It wouldn't be the first time, would it?"

"No," said Wingate. "Where did she go when she left here without Scotty?"

"You mean when she left here?"

"Where did she go?"

"Well," said Whizzer, "I don't know where they went, exactly. To find Blackway, it looks like. Probably they were going up into the Towns, to the place he has up there."

"They?"

"She went with Lester and Nate the Great, there."

"I told her to get Scotty," said Wingate.

"Scotty wasn't here."

"So you said," Wingate said. "You figured Lester and that boy were up to the business?"

"I thought so," said Whizzer. "Nate the Great don't have a lot to say. He don't look like much, but there's more to him than you might think. And Les — well, you know Les."

"I know him," said Wingate.

"Les knows all the tricks."

"He does."

"Come to it, Les'll go all the way through."

"He will."

"Les was willing," Whizzer said. "So was Nate the Great. Scotty wasn't here. And the girl said you told her there was nothing you could do to help her."

"The Towns are out of my district," said Wingate.

"You could have gone in there if you had to, though," said Whizzer. "Couldn't you?"

"What do you think?"

Whizzer nodded.

"She was sitting in her car," Wingate said. "She was sitting in her car with a little knife like you'd use to cut up an apple. If Blackway came after her, she was going to drive him off with a fruit knife."

"She's a pistol," said Whizzer. "Blackway might have picked on the wrong girl, this time, it looks like."

Wingate was silent.

"Did you?" asked Whizzer.

"Did I what?"

"Tell her there was nothing you could do to help her."

"That's right," said Wingate.

"Well, then," said Whizzer, "Somebody ought to done something, it looked like. It wasn't going to be you."

"She wanted me to arrest Blackway because she was afraid he meant to hurt her," said Wingate.

"He did," said Whizzer.

"Maybe he did," said Wingate. "I told her I couldn't arrest somebody for what somebody else thought he meant to do."

"Sure," said Whizzer.

"I told her I couldn't do that," said Wingate, "and she wouldn't want to live in a country where I could. That's a country with no law."

"Sure," said Whizzer.

"Would you?"

"What?"

"Want to live in a country with no law?" Wingate said.

"Well, maybe not," said Whizzer. "But I'll tell you something else: I wouldn't mind living in a country with no Blackway."

"Well," said Wingate, "you do, it looks like. Don't you?"

"I wouldn't be surprised," said Whizzer.

Castle Freeman Jr. is the award-winning author of two previous novels, a story collection, and a collection of essays. He has been a regular essayist for *The Old Farmer's Almanac* since 1982, and lives in Newfane, Vermont.

3